Came a Stranger

Camlachie Nights Trilogy

Book **3**

Marie Rowan

Published Feb 2021
by
Moira Brown
Broughty Ferry
Dundee. DD5 2HZ

ISBN 979-8-7037-6765-8

Dedication:

This book is dedicated to the members of the Montreal Joe Kennaway CSC for all their help and friendship.

Prologue

The girl leaned against the low wall and hoped the feeling of weakness would pass. Was it something she had eaten? Something from that meal last night that had been off? Her hands shook and she made a determined effort to keep hold of both her bags. She walked slowly on, more by instinct than by anything else. The air was cool, a light breeze blowing now and she felt slightly better. Suddenly, it was becoming difficult now to figure out where to put her feet as the ground constantly seemed to move away from her. She knew she had to cross Great Eastern Road with its constant flow of heavy traffic. Should she wait until this light-headedness passed? She stopped for a moment as did the crowd she was now caught up in, then felt herself being swept across the street with the others. She looked up to check where she now was but her eyes would not focus on the sign above. The clamour of people, the sounds of children playing all washed over her, coming and going like an ebbing tide. They were familiar sounds and she smiled gently, then slowly slipped down into eternal oblivion.

Chapter 1

The police constable just gaped open-mouthed at the man speaking to him.

"She just dropped down dead!"

"So you've just said, sir, but that can't be true," the policeman insisted.

"I'm telling you it is. I was walking behind her when she suddenly fell down – dead."

"Dropped dead? Dropped down dead? She looks about twenty and twenty year olds don't drop down dead."

"Well, this one did." Both men gazed upon the pale, lovely face of the dead girl lying on the pavement while the constable waited for help. The deep green, sightless eyes stared up at them, her body slight and small lying pathetically as if at peace. PC Proctor looked away, swallowed hard and busied himself waving away curious onlookers. But his eyes still drifted back to the sad, prone figure lying on the pavement of a busy street in Glasgow's Camlachie district in the East End. Her little dark blue jacket was buttoned tightly over a long black linen dress.

"She's got very small feet." It seemed Proctor was not the only one gazing at the still form of the girl.

"And your name is what, sir?" he asked the man who had watched the girl draw her last breath on earth.

"Ernest Peden." Proctor wrote it down in his notebook.

"And your address, sir?"

"I don't live round here."

"That's not what I asked." Peden paused and his thoughts made some very acrobatic leaps in the one minute it took him to reply.

"29 Airlie Gardens, Bothwell." The constable wrote it all down. He did his best to look inscrutably silent and efficient, but it was hard when his pencil was one inch long and required frequent licking. He refused to risk a total loss of dignity by peeling back the wooden bits hiding the lead.

"No doubt Sergeant Manley will be wanting a statement from you, sir, but we'll see what he has to say when he gets here. Or maybe it'll be Inspector McLachlan." Proctor looked again at the dead girl and thought he would cover her up. But with what? That problem was solved as a cot blanket floated down from on high and landed on his shoulder. He looked up and nodded his thanks to the woman leaning out of the first floor window. The soft crocheted cover was ceremoniously draped over the tragic figure's beautiful face and body and the eyes, still clear as crystal, were gone from sight.

"That's one of the teachers from the school, Mr Proctor. I'm sure it's Miss Colquhoun."

"Aye, that's her alright, Mrs Breslin." The confirmation came from one of the female window-sill-leaners of the third floor of the tenement above them. Proctor hurriedly noted the name and occupation down in his notebook with the same difficulty as before. That teacher must be a new one, he thought, for he knew all of the teachers in that school for years past.

"In East Hope Street," added Mrs Breslin for good measure. Proctor suddenly spotted the girl's bag and satchell peeking out from beneath her dress and hastened to secure them. A crowd had by now built up but were mostly silent. A child began to cry and was unceremoniously hauled back into the closemouth by its mother. Shouts went up, the crowd parted and Proctor was relieved to see Sergeant Manley and some others push their way through to him.

"Dr McPherson was in the police office when your need for help came through and he's come along, Proctor. Should get it all sorted out in double quick time," said Manley. His eyes alighted on the girl as the doctor removed the covering. "Very young, isn't she?" he said. "Any idea who she is?"

"The woman hanging out of the first-floor window says she's a Miss Colquhoun, a teacher in the school in East Hope Street"

"My God, so she is. Mrs Maguire, the heidie, won't like this for it leaves her with a vacancy to fill fast. Very young," he added again, thoughtfully. "Proctor, you and one of the lads who came along with me disperse this crowd. We'll have to get the girl to the morgue as soon as possible, as soon as the doctor says so. These hers?" Manley pointed to the bags and PC Proctor nodded. "I'll take them with me."

"Heart." That was all Dr McPherson said as he stood up. He replaced the covering and came over and stood beside Sergeant Manley. Proctor was good at dispersing crowds and the wagon eased itself alongside the body. "I've seen it before, Bill. Just once or twice. Rare but not that unusual. Probably an unsuspected heart condition, but George Jeffrey will confirm or rubbish that opinion in his usual manner when he does the post mortem. He's seldom satisfied with the the verdict of any doctor who's first called in. An arrogant, young fool. Anyway, the girl's all his now." Who should he inform, thought Manley? Who would be devastated by his news? He would send someone round to the school to inform Mrs Maguire, the headteacher, and would no doubt get some more information from the girl's bags. Teachers were usually orderly in noting down personal information in case of accidents as traffic these days had become almost chaotic in the main thoroughfares of Glasgow. He wondered if he would find a diary and perhaps a clue to that health problem. He watched the wagon tumble away down Society Street and the crowds stop momentarily in respect as it passed. How could that possibly have happened? Teaching one minute and dead the next. And she was really no more than a young girl. It was very depressing, Manley thought, as he began the walk back to Camlachie police office. He would send some of his constables round the tenements in the street and he would interview the man who had seen it happen himself. But, in the meantime, the young lady would be reduced to a mere form in a filing cabinet. He hoped that it was a natural, sudden death, for if not, he would have Ben Pollock and CID his team taking over the station and that meant the place would reek of rolls and sausage night and day. He sighed and kept on walking.

DI Ben Pollock rose from his favourite chair and strode determinedly to the door of his flat. He would soon sort out who thought it acceptable to hammer against it. He threw the door open and then laughed.

"Come in! I should have known it was you. Who's dead and who's mucked up the cause of death?" Dr George Jeffrey barged in past him.

"Shameena out?" he asked roughly.

"Aye."

"Good. Don't want to alarm her."

"You haven't managed that so far, George. Take a seat and get to the point."

"A young teacher's dead and the death was not caused by heart failure. That is to say it was, but not in a natural, malfunctioning way."

"And what does all that blarney mean?" Pollock sat down opposite him by the fire.

"It means it was caused by a rare drug."

"So rare that only you know about it, George?" Dr Jeffrey slumped further into the armchair and wore the expression he always did when he had had an argument with fellow professionals and had come off second best. He was of almost average height, glossy brown hair sleeked back with a pomade of his own concoction, and never seemed to realise it did not work for more than five minutes. All told, the thirty-odd year old pathologist was completely undistinguished-looking except for his eyes that glittered and glistened and were the colour of expensive cognac. They fascinated all who met him. Pollock knew him from his days in India when Jeffrey had got off his ship at the wrong port. The ship had sailed from Bombay without him and it was only because Pollock's regiment was there en route to their regimental headquarters that they had met. Jeffrey had finally managed to reach Hong Kong and then Macao, his original objective. Although Pollock's sceptical reaction to Jeffrey's original pronouncement still stood, he was also well acquainted with the drug involvement of the big Far Eastern companies to realise that Jeffrey would be able to suss out drugs, rare and otherwise, when he came across them.

"It's like this, Ben."

"Hang on, George, tell me from the beginning what this is all about, but mind and leave out all the long and short technical words. And stick to the point. I know they're all incompetent in your eyes. You've told me that dozens of times. Now first, though, George, simmer down and have some tea and cake." Jeffrey strode up and down the kitchen of Pollock's flat, waiting very impatiently for the tea to be poured and the madeira cake sliced. He finally sat down and began talking again and Pollock prepared himself to listen to the last five minutes of a twenty minutes soliloquy which would wander in and out of numerous complaints of victimization, lack of competence in the hospital management team and one of the nurses' rebuffing Jeffrey's well-meant romantic advances. It never varied except for the name of the nurse. But it did that evening.

"Said she was twenty-two years old but they've no proof of that. "

"Who is?"

"Was. The girl who dropped dead in Society Street."

"I presume we're also talking about the police as well as other incompetents?"

"Yes."

"So why have they got no proof? It doesn't always follow that they have, you know, George." Pollock was naturally inclined to stick up for his fellow officers until he knew better.

"There was no identification on the body and the police surgeon's report is an attempt at fiction. Heart attack pure and simple. Some hope! Complete, bloody tripe!"

"Now, now, George, Shameena is only visiting a neighbour across the landing and she has very acute hearing." Jeffrey took the hint.

"It wasn't a heart attack as such."

"But the heart was involved presumably because it just suddenly stopped beating," said Pollock.

"In that case every death is a heart attack. Why bother writing anything else down on a death certificate?"

"I've often wondered that myself, Dr Jeffrey. But, as you've taken the trouble to jump on two different trams either from the Royal Infirmary or from your very spacious and expensive flat in the West End, I'm ready to give you a few minutes of my very valuable time."

"Two trams it was and the flat's rent is hellishly expensive but I need the space and my erstwhile flatmate is now serving a lengthy stretch in Barlinnie for fraud. He is, or was, I suppose, a teller with the Bank of Scotland and evidently not very good at cooking the books. I have to pay his part of the rent now, too."

"That comes of courting a widow with four children who have very expensive needs."

"You're right there, Ben, for she and the brood were a very costly hobby for him but he wouldn't listen."

"And are you still hankering after Sister Wilson? She seems to be acquiring tastes above your own means, George."

"Are you prepared to listen or do I go my own way?" asked the medical man sharply, fully aware that he was almost overdrawn at the bank.

"Please yourself, Dr Jeffrey, as I really don't want to sit and listen to your latest quarrel with your fellow professionals." That always got the pathologist to come to the point.

"This one really was a fight and that's why I'm here. I'll be suspended from duty for punching Dr McPherson on the jaw, so I want you to carry on for me." Pollock sighed for it was not the first time he had heard of Jeffrey's escapades. Jeffrey did not believe in the saying that the pen was mightier than the sword. He had walloped virtually every medical man in Glasgow, it seemed.

"Anything broken?"

"No – as usual. My fist is effective but not lethal."

"If you kept your hands in your pockets and thus avoided fines, that rent wouldn't seem quite so hellish, George. Besides, Mc Pherson's used to it by this time. Think yourself lucky he's your uncle. No official complaints from him. But right now, begin at the end for that way we can save at least fifteen minutes."

"Dr McPherson, Uncle Jim, says it was heart failure of some kind and I say it was the result of the girl taking a rare drug."

"You've excelled yourself, George. I mean in the time-saving department. Now, this far we know that a young woman of roughly twenty-something collapsed and died in Society Street in the East End. When?"

"Yesterday afternoon."

"And we also know that Dr McPherson says heart failure pure and simple for a natural cause, but you say from a rare drug."

"An unknown drug."

"And that is all that is known?"

"Yes, except that she taught in East Hope Street school."

"And why do the police know nothing more about the girl?"

"Because all the information the school holds on her is false. There were no items of a personal nature in her flat, they say, other than clothes and there were very few of them."

"All that from Jim McPherson?"

"That's right. That's what he was told at Camlachie police office."

"Has the death been labelled suspicious?"

“I don’t think so.” Dr Jeffrey took a large bite out of his slice of madeira cake and watched anxiously while Pollock thought it over.

“And what makes you think it’s a rare drug from the Far East?”

“I’ve heard of the symptoms. I didn’t spend a few years in Macao without knowing what was available there for the discerning killer.”

“What symptoms?”

“The way she was conducting herself according to a man who was walking behind her for quite a distance and the way she collapsed.”

“And that’s it?”

“That’s enough.”

“We’ll leave that for the moment as you’re the expert. Now how does a young Glasgow teacher come to be the victim of some Chinese drug plot?” asked Pollock, his voice laced with the scepticism he felt. Jeffrey shrugged.

“I don’t know but I’ll bet everything I own – granted that’s not much – that I’m right.”

“So what, Dr Jeffrey, would you like me, a mere detective inspector with the CID, to do about it? Don’t say prove you’re right for that’s not how it works. I have to be put on the case and, at the moment, you’re telling me that officially there isn’t one. There is also the very important fact that I don’t decide what happened before I begin. In other words, George, you want me to prove you’re right but my job is to seek out the truth and you might not like that. You know how these things work as well as I do. Hire Bell’s Discreet Enquiries.” Pollock’s wife Shameena was an operative with that agency. His feelings regarding this were still somewhat ambivalent.

“I’m skint. At least promise me you’ll make a few enquiries, discreet or otherwise, Ben.”

“I’ll ask a few questions and see where they lead. Don’t you go shouting your mouth off that I’m on the case for there

isn't one and I'm not. And stop assaulting medical men. I presume the medical women are safe?"
"Totally safe."
"So, apart from the fact that you're simply playing a genuine hunch, old friend, there exists no verifiable reason for your thinking as you do?"
"None at all. Only the physical symptoms that girl showed according to the man who was walking directly behind her since she emerged from East Hope Street – the school gates, actually – and was still there when she fell. It was her manner of moving that drew my attention to drugs. The man couldn't stop talking, he was extremely nervous, almost hysterical, that such a thing could happen. And that's about it." Pollock placed another slice of cake on Jeffrey's plate. The only thing in the doctor's life was his work, that and cake of any description and any quality. For some reason or other, he shunned biscuits. Nobody, including Pollock's romantically-inclined wife, Shameena, tried any match-making for Jeffrey was a non-starter. No woman would put up with a husband she never saw, one who made little money, gave most of it away and who also quarreled with every member of the human race he met.
"Alright, George, finish you tea and cake and scarper. I've work to do."
"If you start on this right now, Ben, I'll pay your tram fare to Camlachie."
"Shift yourself, doctor. I'll be taking Jake Jacobstein with me and two tram fares might see you evicted from that ridiculous flat you occupy. We'll make our own way there, unobtrusively, but if you should somehow show up, we'll be sacked and you'll get a good hiding from me. Don't slam the door behind you." Jeffrey did not.

Pollock sat back down again and poured himself some tea. It was stone cold. He rose again, cleaned out the teapot, put tea leaves in it and refilled it from the kettle that swung slowly from an iron hook over the fire. He automatically reached for the cake his mother habitually sent round. A fair exchange for some of Shameena's pakora. What to do? Where to begin? How to avoid being severely reprimanded for interfering, or worse still, being sacked. He heard the front door of his flat being opened and closed and then Shameena was sitting opposite him.

"Was that Dr Jeffrey I saw racing down the stairs, Ben?" Pollock nodded and poured out a cup of tea for his wife.

"Another problem?"

"That man lives for discovering imaginary problems. I really don't know why he came back from Macao for he must have been in his element there. The mysterious East."

"He told me he missed the rain," Shameena informed her husband with a straight face.

"Knowing what a complex mind he has, that might just be true. Couldn't have been that he was simply tired of the heat, the food and the language problems, could it?"

"The language wouldn't have fazed him for he doesn't listen to anyone anyway, Ben. His brain only selects the words he likes and discards the rest."

"Whatever he does, he always acts in one of two ways when he has a problem. He hits any male person who disagrees with him and then lands me with the problem to solve. Right, Shameena, I'm off to send a telegramme to Jake telling him to meet me in Society Street in Camlachie. We'll run the rule over the case that doesn't exist yet and a chat with Bill Manley will tell us all we want to know. Then it will be home and cheerio to Dr George Jeffrey."

Pollock and DS Jake Jacobstein stood looking round them outside 6 Society Street. The air was cool and pleasant, the street almost empty. Glasgow Green would be full of mothers and very young children and folk just enjoying the good weather before the rain that was forecast for later in the week. It might play havoc with the ball and skill on the pitch during the Charity Cup Final at Hampden on the coming Saturday between Celtic and Rangers, but Pollock was certain crowds of supporters would turn up just the same and cause Inspector McLachlan and his men no end of bother in the East End once the game was over. It all suited Pollock very well for McLachlan had delegated Sergeant Hanley to assist Pollock, unofficially of course, and that was why he and Jacobstein were now cooling their heels outside No 6 Society Street. Hanley, being off-duty when contacted by his superior officer, had had little or no choice but to agree to help. He would combine that request of sorts with taking his wife and young children along to the Green and parking them there until he had returned.

"Here he comes, Ben," said Jacobstein as the sergeant hove into sight.

"And what would you gentlemen like me to tell you?" asked Manley after shaking hands and running a practiced eye over the stray pedestrians around them. Old habits died hard. "It's about Miss Colquhoun's death, I take it?" Pollock nodded.

"Inspector McLachlan's told you that this is all unofficial, Bill, I take it?"

"Quite so. Just a quick look to se that all is well, no more, no less." A huge smile spread across the sergeant's face. He had played this game before.

"I expect you could have placed a bet on it, Bill?" Manley nodded.

"When I heard that the pathologist was Dr Jeffrey, yes. Who did he assault this time? His Uncle Jim?"

"My lips are sealed, Bill, but Jake's aren't."

"On his jaw. The good pathologist is a man of very little imagination. Extremely intelligent but sadly lacking in creativity," said Jacobstein.

"His uncle's no better in the imagination department as he seems to get caught within reach every time. Fortunately, Jeffrey's punch is more of a slap. What's he come up with now?"

"An unknown drug."

"From the mysterious East?"

"You've hit the nail right on the head, Bill," said Pollock with mock admiration.

"Then, this time, boys, he might just be right. I was doing the rounds yesterday when it happened. I was standing with one of my constables at the junction of Broad Street and Great Eastern Road when I spotted Miss Colquhoun in a gap in the busy street. I know her only because my eldest is in her class at school. I've met her a few times and she was walking yesterday as if she was in a dream. Not unsteady on her feet, just as if she couldn't actually see where she was putting them. She turned into this street and I lost sight of her. She wasn't staggering or I would have caught up with her in jigtime. She was just very, very slightly hesitant when walking. It's hard to actually describe. It was, I suppose, as if she couldn't quite see clearly. When I heard Dr McPherson say heart failure, I had my doubts. Not that I know anything about that sort of thing. I, Bill Manley, an authority on medical matters that are alcohol induced including the DTs, vomiting and urinating everywhere, found myself silently questioning our police surgeon."

"As she was dead when he was summoned, he hadn't actually seen her walking, Bill?"

"No, he hadn't, nor would he listen to the man who'd been walking behind her since she'd left the school gates. He'll verify my observation and he might yet have a little more to tell under your very astute investigating techniques if you think that Dr Jeffrey and I are right in thinking it all deserves a bit more looking into. The witness's name is Ernest Peden and I've brought you, with almost official permission, the report containing the result of our own investigation. We're Camlachie police office not the library in Landressy Street, so please return it to us within twenty-four hours for that's as long as we can pretend to higher authorities that we've mislaid it should any enquiries about it come to us." Manley handed over a slim folder containing the report which had been in his notecase. "Sorry there's not much there, Ben. The best of luck and watch that jaw of yours if your conclusions differ in any way from those of the mad medic."

"Take another minute to tell us what you know already, Bill, then we'll have a seat in your Camlachie cells and study the report. Should be able to let you have it back straight away and let you sleep easy tonight."

"As I said, not much to go on. Plenty of surprises, too many in fact, but all negative. It's the most unusual case I've ever known. It's more or less been put on the back burner as the official cause of death is heart failure. No need, therefore, to take it any further. Odd circumstances but nothing actually illegal or criminal except some false papers and that's now dead and gone with the girl's death. We first of all searched her bags that she had with her in the street. The usual things in both but absolutely nothing personal. The satchell just held school jotters to be marked. There was nothing with a name and address or anything that could lead us to identifying the dead girl. If she hadn't taught in the local school, we'd have been completely stymied. We got some information from the head-teacher, that is to say the home address they held, and this morning we contacted the education department. Enquiries have since revealed that her teaching qualifications are excellent but false. I sent some of the lads round to where she stayed. A bit out of our area but everybody's busy and nobody minded as it was just really a simple follow-up to a death from natural causes."

"No luck, I take it, Bill?" said Pollock.

"Exactly. She did live there but, yet again, the place seemed completely sterile. Clothes, soap and hairwash, very little food but it is possible to eat there anyway if the residents pay for it. It looked as if she only had breakfast there and a meagre one at that. She wasn't undernourished so she probably ate elsewhere. It seems she ate her dinner in school, brought it in herself, we were told. She seldom talked to the rest of the staff and avoided the staff-room.

Not very sociable. She was a conscientious teacher, so it seems. That's about it, Ben. Not much for you to go on, as I said."

"So we really only know her name and address and what she might have died of, and, of those three, her name was probably false. Wish I'd kept the door shut on that pathologist!" Jake Jacobstein laughed and rubbed his hands together.

"This is one for the mystery aficionados, Ben," he said smiling.

"Like you, Jake?"

"Made for me."

"Then let's go. We'll be in touch, Bill." Pollock had a quick look at the folder. " Right now we're heading for a Miss Andrea Colquhoun's digs in Bosworth Street it says on the outside of this file, a house along at Tollcross where DS Jacobstein will no doubt solve the puzzle the minute he enters the building. I expect the newspapers have reported this as a natural death. My copies are still lying around at home unread only by Shameena. Too many reports to write."

"There's just a line or two about a teacher and a suspected heart attack. I wouldn't expect any follow-up unless the two of you can bring a rabbit out of a hat. But as your investigation is unofficial, we'll probably hear no more about it. It will all really die a natural death as well."

"And George Jeffrey will no longer be welcome in my home. Be seeing you, Bill." And with that and the folder tucked safely under his arm, Pollock headed for 17 Bosworth Street, Tollcross.

Bosworth Street was a long row of terraced town houses which had seen better days. Genteel poverty was knocking at most of the doors. Fine droplets of sudden rain had cleared the street but Pollock had the feeling that this one did not see much in the way of traffic or pedestrians out for a stroll anyway. It was clean, tidy and inexorably on the way down the social scale although with a bit of money ploughed into it, a very different clientele might have been more than anxious to abide there. He also felt that dinner would be uniformly cold and grey and on a white plate but the cutlery would be top notch. He always felt sad when faced with people valiantly swimming slowly through adversity, almost drowning in it, but determined to make the most of what remained of a happier and more successful financial past. He never mocked the lonely ladies who kept these boarding houses well turned out, the flag-stones leading up to the front doors immaculate, the brass door-knockers gleaming brightly in the weak sunlight. Pollock somehow felt his spirits lifting.

Jake Jacobstein banged the lion-headed knocker and both CID men stood back and waited. The silence was broken by the sound of footsteps marching determinedly through from, presumably, the kitchen at the back. The door was thrown open and the exact opposite of a mild-mannered, genteel lady, impoverished but proud, opened the door.

"CID? Saw you coming along the street. Just been putting the kettle on. Come in!"

"Thank you, sir." Pollock smiled at the 6 feet image of a young, fit man as he stepped past him and into the sweet-smelling hall. A somewhat bemused Jacobstein stepped in after him and both followed the man into an airy and well-equipped kitchen. Warrant cards were produced.

"All right, folks, I admit it. I killed the impoverished landlady after ten years of indifferent cooking and stuffed her under her bed."

"Thank you, sir, we'll send someone round in a month or so to take down your confession. You can keep the body, sir, until the next rent is due. After that, I promise you we'll review your case. Just milk in my tea, sir. Thank you." Pollock knew a great cup of tea when he tasted one, the shortbread was like balm to him.

"And what is your name, sir?" asked Jacobstein, helping himself to a chocolate biscuit.

"Peter Yair, owner of this humble but sylish abode. Inherited it last year from my aunt who had already established a reputation for clean beds and good cuisine. The clean beds are still with us but not the good cuisine. Bed and beakfast only unless a meal is bought and paid for and ordered a week in advance. I can't stand the smell of cabbage and the residents don't like my Irish stew. Nothing to do with wanting money up-front, just that I need a week to learn how to cook whatever the residents request. However, I've enrolled in a course of traditional, non-smelly cooking at the Perthshire House School of Culinary Arts in the Gorbals run by a friend of mine as I intend turning my immaculate front garden into a high-class baking outlet. Change of usage. A tearoom cum bakers."
"And the best of luck, Mr Yair," said Jacobstein.
"Actually, I've just had the builders in to price the outside. Likewise the architect. Did the inside myself in a small way. Still got the residents so don't want to upset them at the moment. My aunt was genteel but definitely not impoverished though she liked to act the part. She only took in lodgers who added tone to the place."
"Inherited her money as well, did you, sir?" asked Pollock.
"The entire estate." The man smiled broadly and Pollock wondered why he was one of millions who had no relatives who were well-heeled. Ah well. He sighed and just got on with it.
"And did Miss Colquhoun add to the tone of this place?"
"She most certainly did, Inspector Pollock."
"Well, Mr Yair, it's Miss Colquhoun we've come about. We'd like to see her room but before we do that, can you tell us a little about her as a person, how and why she chose your house to live in? Any friends or acquaintances of any kind who visited her?" Pollock finished his tea and shortbread and waited hopefully.
"I can tell you very little , inspector," said Yair, shaking his head, "for I only came back here in November when my

aunt died and Miss Colquhoun was already here. My aunt might have known more but I don't think so. The lovely lady teacher was very close-mouthed. There were one or two visitors – male – who came and went. Just talked in the common-room on the left as you come in. House rules, it seems, from way back. I only opened the door to them for Miss Colquhoun was already waiting for them at the foot of the stairs. She showed them out. It happened about three or four times, just for your records. All quiet, no voices raised, seemed to be good friends, maybe relatives. Can't describe them as they were totally ordinary people."

"And when was this, Mr Yair?" asked Jacobstein.

"End of November, then St Valentine's Day and on St Patrick's Day. I know the days because we baked special cakes at the Perthshire for these special occasions. I had some friends round for a special Irish meal. The one and only time I've cooked Irish stew. It was pathetic but the cake and drink were quality and plentiful. Miss Colquhoun gave me a withering look as she showed her guests out. And that's it. I don't think I ever heard her speak."

"We'd like to have a look at her room now, sir."

"Here's the key, Inspector Pollock. I'm in here if you need me."

Pollock and Jacobstein climbed the stairs and found Room 5 at the end of a short corridor. The room was very clean and tidy and had obviously been the recipient of Peter Yair's deep-cleaning attentions. The bed was not made up but was covered with a pristine white spread, edged with small squares of different colours. The pillow cases were of the same set. A wardrobe and matching dresser stood side by side and bedside tables were placed on either side of the double bed with matching lamps on top. A chest of drawers completed the furniture which was of rosewood throughout. Mr Yair's aunt had obviously known better times. She had once graced the social ladder from a much greater height and had kept her furniture with her on her travels. Jacobstein had an eye for quality and was very impressed.

"Wasted in a boarding-house. I wonder if he wants to sell any of it?"

"As we're here unofficially, Jake, feel free to ask him. He'll need all the money he can get to start up this new business venture." They were both searching the room thoroughly as they spoke. The girl's belongings had not yet been packed away. Pollock stepped outside for a moment.

"Mr Yair, a minute, please." Pollock and Jacobstein waited as Yair ran lightly up the deep carpeted stairs and joined them.

"When did you clean this place?" Pollock asked looking at the dust-free zone.

"I didn't. A very fussy lady does the rooms for me. She'd been with my aunt for a long time and then simply transferred her allegiance to me. Very particular, she is."

"So nothing has been changed?"

"Nothing, I presume, if your officers put it all back as they found it. But I might add, too, that I never enter my residents' rooms. I will also add that my cleaning lady does not usually do this room by order of the late occupant. This very sterile atmosphere is all Miss Colquhoun's doing. Can you see yourselves out, gentlemen? I'm in the early stages of making a soufle – my cookery school homework. This is a trial run and I think I'm about to fail. By the way, I found this in a drawer in the hall table. The cleaner must have picked it up off the floor and put it there." With that, Peter Yair vanished.

"Jake, I think you and I will test the new tea-shop when it opens. Mr Yair deserves to succeed."

"And maybe his success will rub off on us, Ben. This book he handed to us on his way downstairs."

"Poetry. Is he trying to sell it? Do you even like poetry, Jake?" asked Pollock jokingly.

"I can take it or leave it. I suspect he thinks that it might belong to the late Miss Colquhoun," Jacobstein mused as he opened it. "And, Ben, I think he might be right."

"Name? Initials? If so, this will be the first personal item we've found – or anyone else, for that matter." But Jacobstein just shook his head.

"No name, no initials. But look at this." Jacobstein handed Pollock an embroidered, silk bookmark and Pollock turned it over slowly in his hand.

"The Year of the Tiger. Now, Jake, I know that was 1878-79 for a Chinese couple who are friends of Shameena had a baby in that year. And do you know what that year is? No? It is the year of leaders and rebels. Jeffrey was almost certainly right. The Far East connection is alive and well and deadly here in Glasgow."

Chapter 2

Ben Pollock stepped off the tram, crossed Great Eastern Road and entered Camlachie police office the following morning. Inspector Mclachlan gave him a wry smile.

"Can't thank you enough for taking this case off our hands, Ben."

"It's a time-limited job, I'm afraid. Somebody's got friends in high places, it seems, for from the minute I suggested that I have a quick look into it officially, my superintendent thought Chrismas had come early. But I've only got three days or so to look into it and either solve it or decide it's not a homicide." They both wondered who had the influential friend.

"My office as usual?" asked McLachlan.

"If you don't mind. Think I've still got some biscuits in my tin so the kettle will go on first. Any of my team here yet?"

"Jake Jacobstein. Austin Quigley's gone for some pies from Dough Frae Me's. Be back any minute."

"Lovely. Now that's put me in a good mood and I'll be rarin' to go after a round-the-table catch-up." With that, Pollock took the stairs two at a time and entered the office that had recently become a favourite of his. A South-side boy himself, he reluctantly acknowledged the East End had just about everything on his 'favourites' list; great butchers, bakers, pubs and a few really good restaurants. That was as far as he looked. A clatter of running footsteps behind him and he turned as Austin Quigley, his detective constable, kicked the office door open, a cardboard box full of pies claiming the attention of his hands.

"Hot as hell, sir, just out the oven." That was the last of the talk as the three men set about the tea and pies, Jacobstein's potato one looking decidedly peely-wally in Pollock's eyes.

"Have a biscuit or two, Jake, or that cheese bagel." Jacobstein helped himself to both and, replete, the three men congregated round the desk as Ben Pollock helped himself to some of McLachlan's stack of blue, foolscap notepaper.

"Right, then, a summimg-up of the case. We're here today to begin, officially, enquiries into the death of Miss Andrea Colquhoun. We've been given roughly three days or so to sum up the case before it's closed down for good if it doesn't, in our eyes, warrant further investigation. We've got a bit of a headstart because Jake and I have done a bit of unofficial sleuthing already as you now know, Austin. Now, if we find nothing suspicious, the case will be closed down or put on the back-burner in case something turns up later on. There will be no more time spent on it. This next bit is for Austin's information. A young teacher died suddenly on the pavement in Society Street the day before yesterday. We know her name, address and that she taught in East Hope Street school. According to Sergeant Manley of this police office, his men have been unable to find any belongings of hers that would give any additional information on her. Jake and I have spoken to the landlord of her lodgings and he knows nothing at all about her. We're only investigating this because Dr George Jeffrey has queried Dr McPherson's cause of death. McPherson thinks it was simply heart failure while Jeffrey thinks it was a poison of a mysterious Far Eastern origin. Yes, I know, we've all been here before. The school the woman taught in knows no more than her address and qualifications for teaching. Sergeant Manley and the man who was walking behind the deceased both noticed a slight hesitancy in the way she was walking. Manley had seen her a few times at the same time of day and insists that there was something not quite right about her just before she died. One of his children was in her class and he was on speaking terms with her. The only other piece of evidence that we have was given to Jake and me when we went to her digs in Bosworth Street. This is it." Pollock produced from a large manila envelope the small poetry book complete with its bookmark with the image of a tiger"

"What's that?" asked Quigley, eyeing it closely.

"It's a bookmark, Austin. Some people use them to hold their page for them unlike the vast majority of Scotland's population who use a torn piece of the Daily Record or, if they are more affluent and don't need all of the newspaper for lavatory purposes, a betting slip. The important part of this is that the image denotes the Year of the Tiger with the date 1878-79. The Chinese people give every year the name of an animal and their year runs from February till January. This might just tie in with Dr Jeffrey's Far East poison. That is what makes it important." Pollock stopped and flicked through the book again. "I can find no passage marked, so I take it Miss Colquhoun was simply a lover of Yeats' poems."

"Has the teacher been formally identified yet, Inspector Pollock?"

"By the headteacher, yes. As we've had no relatives contacting us so far, it looks like we'll have to make do with that."

"I can't understand why there are no personal effects in either her purse or her room at Tollcross, Ben," commented Jacobstein, clearing away the mugs. Quigley rose and took them out into the corridor to rinse them out. There was a thoughtful silence until he came back.

"Well," said Pollock at last, "we have to decide upon our next move right now for time is moving along very quickly and this might just be a murder case. What do we really need to find out in order of importance. Top priority is to be given to what?"

"Who is Andrea Coquhoun?" suggested Jacobstein

"Is the body really that of Miss Colquhoun?" countered Pollock.

"Headteacher says so," said Quigley, who was still young enough to think that that opinion should never be questioned.

"But does she know that for certain?" asked Jacobstein, "or is she assuming that's who the deceased is because a few certificates say so?"

"You've got a very valid point there, Jake. I wonder if the young lady's school colleagues have heard anything from her own lips that suggest otherwise," said the inspector thoughtfully.

"If they have, none of them mentioned it to Inspector McLachlan's men. There's nothing of that in their report." Jacobstein scanned it as he spoke.

"If I remember correctly, Jake, they didn't list the names of the teachers they interviewed. Maybe some have been missed out. Austin, would you check that out right now with Sergeant Manley?" Quigley exited at his usual rate of knots.

"Also, Ben, there's no mention of anybody speaking to the janitor, the most important person in the building, and definitely never coming across as the heidie's best friend. Conversations tend to be very relaxed ones with the janny."

"An excellent point. We must also remember that this investigation is still at the very earliest stage and nobody involved in this report is looking at the girl's death as anything other than from natural causes. That's what it says on the formal death certificate as it stands at the moment."

"Nobody except us!"

"Right, Jake, and Dr Jeffrey. And speak of the devil." All eyes were now on the door, awaiting it being flung open to the wall. "Come away in, Dr Jeffrey. We heard your voice as did everyone, we suspect, living from The Tron to Bridgeton Cross."

"Alright, alright. You've made your point, Ben. Any arrest made yet?"

"Have you identified the poison yet? Have you even discovered traces of a poison yet?"

"Well, no."

"Then that's the same answer to your question," said Pollock, passing the biscuit tin to Jeffrey. He shook his head as was expected and Jacobstein put it away. "We have no case to investigate without proof the lady was poisoned. We're conducting an enquiry here but it's based solely on conjecture and that would certainly be chucked back to us poste haste should we ever get the length of submitting it to the Procurator Fiscal. We have three days and that's our lot and yours, too, George, and that's only because someone was very good at leaning heavily on the higher-up boys. Instead of being here bawling the odds, mate, you should be in your laboratory finding the truth and proof of that girl's death. We'll go on the assumption that you're right, but it all falls to the ground if you can't substantiate your iffy conclusions. So, back off and let us get on with finding out whatever we can in a most complex case. As far as we're concerned as of now, all that girl left behind her, by way of personal information, was precisely nothing. Her teaching qualifications were false. The education department have had another closer look at them and it appears that the dates have been altered. There is no record of her ever having worked in Scotland before although she told the headteacher otherwise. There was nothing in her digs you could call informative and equally nothing was learned from her landlord. That's what we've got to go on. This entire enquiry, and possibly our jobs, hinges on your ability to put your money where your mouth is. Name that poison if it indeed exists. We have just a very slender piece of evidence, and I'm using that word very loosely indeed, and it's this. A bookmark which was found in a book which we think might have been hers."
"What does it look like?" asked Jeffrey.
"A proper bookmark, embroidered. She evidently shunned the local newspaper or baulked at turning down the top corner of the book. The image is of a tiger and the date is 1878-79."

"It's Chinese then?"

"Dr Jeffrey, those nasty rumours that you only listen to your own voice are palpably untrue."

"Cut the sarcasm, Ben. There's your link."

"And the Year of the Tiger is also the one of all rebels. Are we up against a group of Chinese insurgents, a girl with Chinese connections or damn all, and she's just seen it in a second-hand shop, liked it and bought it?" But Jeffrey was a man with a mission alright.

"Or Hong Kong. She might have a connection with Hong Kong. Army, or a trading relative." The pathologist was now cock-a-hoop that there might be a link that would bolster his Far East poison theory.

"So, unless we find out who she actually was, it's all speculation. We'll do our best to give her her real name, George."

"You won't do that by sitting here eating mutton pies. I could smell them a mile off."

"And a mile off is where you'd better stay if you don't want me to stymie your somewhat troubled career. The flaws you've experienced so far could suddenly mushroom and you would find yourself likely to be offered the post of bedpan emptier at the Royal. I'm not saying that I'd deliberately pile the blame for wasting police time on you, but circumstances and self-preservation might just compel me to do it." Pollock sat back, folded his arms and waited.

"You win. I'll go back right now and find it." Dr Jeffrey stopped at the door of the office. "Which poem was it marking?"

"Get to hell out of here, George, and get to work." The door slammed but Austin Quigley slipped in just in time.

"Three teachers and the janny were all off the premises when the boys in blue were there." Quigley put the list in front of his boss.

"Then we'll interview them. Jake, you're the literary man in this group."

"Me?" interrupted a surprised and suspicious Jacobstein, "since when?"

"Since that book of poems happens to be at your side of the desk. We left the bookmark exactly as we found it, so look and see what the poem is on that page or pages." Jacbstein took up the little green, leather-bound book and cautiously fingered his way through it.

"Here it is. The poem's called 'The Host of the Air' and it seems to be about a man having a hard time keeping the young bloods away from his intended bride. Just skimmed through it. But it's Irish, not Chinese."

"Don't suppose the bride's name was Andrea Colquhoun?" asked Pollock hopefully.

"Bridget and I don't think WB Yeats would fancy being arrested."

"Might upset the Charity Cup Final if we tried it," commented Quigley and then wished he had stayed silent. Jacobstein continued.

"The other page is 'Lines written in Dejection'. I quote, 'I have nothing but the embittered sun. Banished heroic mother moon and vanished."

"That's it! Close it! Enough's enough! Let's get the real work done. Jake, you and I are off to school again. We'll interview the three missing teachers and the janny. Names, please?"

"Mrs Newall, Miss Alerdyce and Miss Templeton. The janny is a Mr Ford McCubbin, ex HLI." Pollock took the list from Quigley and placed it in his notebook.

"Right, now, Austin, you take this precious piece of possible evidence, namely the bookmark, along the street to Jacobstein's American Emporium and speak to whoever's in charge of stationery."

"That'll be Mr David Smollet," said Jake Jacobstein, a scion of the family who owned the huge department store.

"Then show it to Mr Smollet and let him give it the once-over and listen carefully to what he thinks. Don't let him sell you anything! I can't put that on expenses and you've got enough pencils to last you for your entire career in the police force." It was well-known Quigley was unable to resist the soft sell.

"I love stationery shops or even just stationery departments," said Quigley as he watched Pollock carefully place the Year of the Tiger bookmark inside a thick envelope.

"Guard this with your life, Austin, for it might just be the solution to this investigation or it might just as easily be nothing at all."

"Trust me, sir." Off went Quigley with the scent of expensive paper and pens in his nostrils. He promised himself he would have a quick look at the pencils while he was there.

"And you and I, Jake, are going to stroll down memory lane, the primary school one, my lad, and no quaking when we're invited into the headteacher's office."

"Three teachers and the janny."

"And all before dinner-time. We've got the list and we'll put them through the mill just for old times' sake. Jake, we now have the opportunity that every boy dreams of but never actually gets, so let's make the most of it. Personally I'm going to extract my own revenge by refusing to stand up straight with my arms by my side."

"Hands in your pockets, Ben?"

"Well, that's maybe carrying it a bit too far. But I might even lean very slightly against a wall."

But, in the event, Pollock did not. He had stood up straight, held his notebook in one hand and a pencil in the other by his sides. Jacobstein had leaned lightly against the nearest wall and had difficulty suppressing a grin.

"Start from the highest classroom and work your way down," the janny had advised. Mrs Daphne Newall had met them at the door of her classroom having refused to leave it in order to be interviewed in the empty medical-room. Reasons were not forthcoming and the CID men had trundled up three plus flights of very steep stairs to her room. Her most welcoming smile, if she possessed one, made no appearances while they were there. The inspector was cheered by the fact that he could leave the room any time he liked as no permission was required and a stern warning to return from the boys' toilet in double quick time would not be heard. Warrant cards to the fore. A look of contempt greeted them and Pollock decided to put the boot in where it would hurt most. Her vanity.

"It's with heavy hearts we find ourselves here, Mrs Newell, for it seems quite inexplicable to my sergeant, DS Jacobstein, and me that a teacher could be working in a school and yet virtually nothing is known about her." His sympathetic tone of voice was recognised as a mild chastisement.

"And what aught I to know about her? You will realise that I am not speaking on behalf of my colleagues."

"I would imagine that it would be extremely difficult to sit in a staff-room day by day without some social chit-chat taking place. Common courtesy, I would have thought," said Pollock somehow feeling he was on a hiding to nothing here. "Miss Colquhoun was a very young teacher, a very new member of staff, and that alone might have aroused some sort of, shall we say, motherly feelings, in the older members of staff." Jacobstein had the feeling his boss had not so much satisfied his boyish feelings of revenge as blown them completely.

"As older members of staff are more cognisant of their responsibilities to the employers who pay their salaries, they keep their minds strictly on their duties to their jobs."

"Highly commendable, Mrs Newell, and I'm sure the parents of all the children attending this school will no doubt appreciate that. But, correct me if I'm wrong, Mrs Newell, I'm under the impression that no talking about school matters is encouraged in any school staffroom in Glasgow. A means of relaxation from the heavy pressures of teaching, I've been told." A long silence followed this last comment.

Pollock and Jacobstein waited, Pollock feeling he had won a watch and Jacobstein wondering where he had got that bit of information. The lady heaved her formidable bosom and looked down at the pile of jotters on her desk. There would be no shortage of red pencils in that classroom, thought Jacobstein, Mrs Newell would see to that. The teacher drew in a deep breath and spoke.

"You are correct, Inspector Pollock."

"Then did you at any time speak to Miss Colquhoun about non-school matters?" he asked.

"I did."

"Would you like to expand on that, please?"

"I told her to remove her packet of biscuits from the cupboard in the staffroom. We all contribute a set sum of money for tea-biscuits per week and told her she either joined the list or kept her biscuits to herself and in a cupboard in her own room."

"Did she intend sharing them for free?"

"Yes, I believe she did. That sort of thing breeds competition and before we know what's happening, the younger teachers would be competing with each other in making cakes and the like with money they could actually be saving. That's how a downward spiral into debt begins, officers."

"Quite so, Mrs Newell, quite so. The frivolous spending of a penny or two on an iced biscuit could easily have led to the ignominy of bankruptcy. She must have thanked you for setting her straight." Mrs Newell's outraged expression told the truth of that one.

"Not quite. I have no intentions of repeating her insulting language."

"Fiery, was she?"

"I'll say. Gutter language with a bit of Liverpool vowels appearing. My husband, Mr Arthur Newell, is in shipping, and I sometimes accompany him on business trips there during school holidays. And that was that as far as conversation or verbal battles were concerned. I happened to notice that she liked to quote WB Yeats' poetry, so perhaps she was from a Liverpool Irish family." Ben Pollock had now fallen in love with the scholastic dragon. The area abounded with Irish families. Maybe that was the group they should be targeting, he thought.

"Well, our thanks for all you help, Mrs Newall." The teacher said nothing more but they were very conscious of her eyes on them all the way down to the ground floor. They paused at the foot of the stairs to quickly confer. Jamie Dalbrenko's name was on each man's lips. There was nothing Jamie did not know about the Irish families thereabouts. He sang round the backcourts of the massive number of tenements in the district for a living of sorts, and officially made a small fortune selling bicycle parts in his spare time. It cheered up both CID officers to realise that they had passed Jamie not thirty minutes before as he had sat looking dejected in the front vestibule at Camlachie police office. He was a bookie's runner and had obviously been caught unable to run as fast as some of the worst horses his clients were betting on.

"Who's next, Jake?"

"Miss Alerdyce. Mr McCubbin, the janny, says she's responsible for keep fit, so, it's the gym for us and that sign says 'Gym This Way'."

The morning interval had just begun and Pollock hoped to catch all three teachers during that break. He hoped that Miss Alerdyce was particular at tidying up and had not gone off yet to savour her prescribed tea and tea-biscuit."

"Here she is, Ben," said Jacobstein quietly as he nudged his superior officer in a most insubordinate way. The very lovely Miss Alerdyce approached. Warrant cards were shown.

"CID?" she asked smiling. The speechless CID just nodded.

"I know nothing. Didn't like her by instinct. Said the

teaching profession was populated by a lot of frustrated old maids who hated children and that my job was worse than useless as the children got more exercise in the streets than in my gym." With that, the very lovely Miss Alerdyce swept by as the CID men admired every movement, subtle or otherwise, of her beautiful body." Pollock, the married man, recovered first.

"Who's next, Jake?" Jacobstein suddenly realised he was not in heaven but in the land of the living. He reached for his copy of the list.

"Working-class, maybe Liverpool Irish. That's it so far," he complained as he searched his notebook for the list. "What a total waste of time this has been."

"So you call that encounter a waste of time, Jake? I despair of you."

"That last one was simply a bonus, Ben. Unfortunately," he added quietly.

"Now, who's the last of the Odd Bods? Hope this one's more average than the rest." But their luck was right out that day in that department.

Mrs Templeton was the harassed mother of five children all under nine years of age and married to an inveterate but unsuccessful gambler. Sergeant Manley had warned Pollock but it had slipped his mind. Her mind was scarcely on her job and life at school was a series of stressful interviews in the head-teacher's office. Pollock made the usual introductions.

"I thought the classroom would be quiet during playtime," she explained. "Always teachers on the go, in and out of everywhere at the interval. What is it you want to speak to me about?"

"We're speaking to all the teachers in this school, not just you, Mrs Templeton. The police officers from Camlachie police office came here too late to speak to everyone, so my sergeant and I are here to complete the list. After we've spoken to you, we've only to see the janitor, Mr McCubbin."

"He's gone out. Official business – probably," said Mrs Templeton in a very resigned manner. "The Camlachie Burn Inn I believe it's called. But why are you interviewing the staff of this school, inspector? Somebody stolen the chalk?" Pollock smiled weakly.
"We're making enquiries concerning the sudden death of one of your colleagues, Mrs Templeton."
"A death? That's impossible. Well, no, of course it isn't. I've been in here all morning. Who on earth can it be?"
"Miss Andrea Colquhoun." Mrs Templeton's face blanched and she slumped down heavily into her chair behind the desk. Tears welled up in her dark blue eyes, then spilled and trickled slowly down her freckled cheeks. "Oh, no, not Andrea." This was the first show of emotion that the girl's death had evoked and the two men waited patiently until the infant teacher had recovered.
"Would you like some water, Mrs Templeton?" Jacobstein asked.
"No, son, I'm alright. It's just such a great shock. Andrea was such a well-meaning girl. Wasn't the best teacher in the world but she tried and was never too proud to ask me for advice. Her classroom's just round the corner. My God, I can't believe this. This is my first day back this week. Broken arm. Nobody came and told me. What a lot of rats they really are! Andrea sorted a few of them out." Mrs Templeton burst into tears again.
"I'm so sorry to have been the bearer of bad news," said Pollock and to his horror, had a hard time keeping his voice from breaking down.
"You can't help that or the boy there either." Mrs Templeton looked almost four years older than Jacobstein. "How can I help?" She dried her eyes yet again on her sleeve and sighed deeply.
"How well did you know Miss Colquhoun? And how long, too, might help?"

"Just since she started some months ago. We hit it off right away. You see, inspector, my husband is a gambler. Addicted to it and monstrously bad at it so I'm really the bread-winner for him, me and the five off-spring. The situation causes much, and I might add, extremely hurtful comment within the staff here but I need the job. When young Andrea came along, I was suddenly not alone. She heard the talk, gave her opinion of the staff to the staff and we became firm friends. But I really only had time to speak to her about teaching. Oddly enough, we both live – lived – in Bosworth Street and she sometimes would come out and play with the children. She was very generous with money in a quiet sort of way. You know, sweeties and little toys and games for them. Nothing expensive but very welcome. But now that I think of it, she never actually talked about herself. When did she die? When did it happen?"

"Miss Colquhoun left the school the day before yesterday, going exactly where, we don't know. Could have been shopping, anything. She turned into Society Street and suddenly dropped to the ground, dead. Heart failure, we think, but that is still ongoing. As it was a sudden death of a very young person, we're making more enquiries than usual. Just ensuring everything is in order. Sudden death means a little more work for the medical men."

"I can't believe that a healthy young girl would suddenly drop dead." Mrs Templeton was having a hard time coming to terms with the news.

"I can assure you, Mrs Templeton, that it's not uncommon. There are many heart conditions that only death throws up. It's always extremely sad and distressing for those involved. But our problem is we haven't been able to find anything among Miss Colquhoun's possessions that give us any information about her family. We were hoping that you might be able to help us."

"A name even would help us a lot," put in Jacobstein.

"The Reverend Alan Carson of the Jerusalem Missionary Society. They send missionaries to China. In fact, he's an ex-missionary himself. I saw him speaking to her outside the gates on Tuesday. Just rushed past them as I was in a bit of a hurry. I had come in to deliver a letter from my doctor stating my arm was fine and that I could resume my teaching duties today. You'll find him in the church mission hall in Lavender Street." Pollock and Jacobstein could not for a moment believe their luck. They thanked Mrs Templeton and the headteacher before leaving the school. As they clanged the school gates shut behind them, Austin Quigley came hurrying up.

"If he's bought a single pencil from your department store, Jake, I'll ram it up his nose."

"If you do, David Smollet won't take it back and give him a refund."

"So, how goes it, Austin?" Pollock's eyes carefully scanned Quigley's jacket looking for writing implement bulges.

"Sir, Peter Yair's been attacked and left for dead."

Chapter 3

Pollock remained stoney-faced for the rest of the tramride into the City Centre and Jacobstein knew better than to intrude on his thoughts. They walked up the steep hill of the ancient High Street, past the centuries old and beautiful building of the Cathedral, giving the Necropolis on their right barely a glance before turning in through the gates of The Royal Infirmary.

"You do the talking, Jake. I'm trying to figure this whole thing out from what little we know about any of the folk in your revered notebook. If George Jeffrey appears, you tell him to sod off and I'll simply ignore him. That wee swine kicked all this off then backed away into his laboratory."

"You told him to, Ben."

"Don't quibble."

"Fine by me. I'll tell the matron you've lost your voice."

"That's good enough, Jake, now here she comes. Make it short and sweet. Ask to see Yair and if he's said anything. That done, we're out of here and back to Camlachie police office. I've told Austin to fetch the Reverend Alan Carson back there. Hope he doesn't come before we've eaten for I'm absolutely starving. Wonder whether Mr Yair's attack was random or he was targeted?" Pollock stopped talking, tried not to look intimidated, and wondered how a bout of laryngitis might affect his face. A mournful, wan smile should do the trick, he reckoned. It did not – again.

"What is it this time, Inspector Pollock? Sore throat, toothache, hammer toes? Some rare condition that's stopping you addressing me?" Her voice boomed along the long, cold corridor.

"Goodness no, Matron. You certainly have a lively imagination. I hope you realise that the short."

"Very short," said Matron decisively.

"Conversations we have are invariably the highlight of my day," said Pollock without blushing.

"What conversations? Jacobstein and I talk, you listen. So, what's new today?"
"The reason for our presence in this building, Matron, is that DS Jacobstein is always pleading with me to give him more responsibility, let him have his head, so to speak."
"Liar! Fire away, DS Jacobstein. I take it you're enquiring about Mr Peter Yair?"
"We are, Matron. First of all, how is he?"
"Unconscious. I could give you some technical terms but that is what it amounts to. The report on his condition and injuries has already been sent to Camlachie police office as they seem to be handling the assault."
"We're on our way there when we leave here, Matron. Thank you. Do you think we could see him? Maybe he's come round in the last few minutes?" Jacobstein lived in hope, Pollock didn't. Matron turned back to Pollock.
"Your sergeant makes no more sense than you do, Inspector Pollock." With that, Matron Carberry turned on her heel and marched back the way she had come.
The two CID men relaxed once they were back in the High Street.
"Efficient, Jake, that's what that lady is, efficient and terrifying. And you thought Mrs Newell was somewhat formidable. That matron has me in a cold sweat at the very thought of speaking to her. She brushed me aside like swatting a fly. Still, we'll get the report and also one from Sergeant Manley concerning the actual assault itself."
"Odd, isn't it, that it would be him?" Jacobstein ran and jumped onto the tram that rumbled its way along to Parkhead. Pollock joined him.
"As you know, I'm not a great believer in coincidences. We'll keep an open mind on it and go back there and question him when he regains consciousness. If the Reverend Carson is not at Camlachie, we'll have a spot of dinner in your store's restaurant – using your staff discount card, of course, - and then make our way back to the office

and speak to him. We're running around here like bumble bees and for what? One dubious death from natural causes and one assault. Taken separately and together, they don't add up to a hill of beans in a city of eight hundred thousand citizens." Pollock hoped that the Reverend Carson would not be there yet. He was bound to be disappointed.

As they entered the police office, Sergeant Bill Manley took time out from pacifying a mother whose child had been spoken to by a policeman for playing football in the street. The woman's voice could have split rock and her anger and fury knew no bounds. She looked at Pollock in mid-stream, recognized him and thought better of including him in her diatribe on policemen in general and the CID in particular. The child was immediately hauled outside and presumably back to school.

"Another satisfied customer, Bill?" Pollock suggested and turned to look in the direction Manley's finger pointed. In amongst half the population of the East End it seemed, sat a clergyman and Pollock said goodbye to his dinner.

"Mr Carson, this is Detective Inspector Pollock who wishes to have a word with you," said Manley and watched as the three men took the stairs leading to Pollock's temporary office. General chitchat, several cups of tea, a few biscuits and they were ready to go.

"Mr Carson, we're investigating the death of someone I'm led to believe you knew, Miss Andrea Colquhoun."

"So I've been told, Inspector Pollock, but I just don't believe it."

"I think I can safely say you're not the only one, Mr Carson, for that seems to be the reaction of everyone I've met so far. She was very young to have died from heart failure and that seems to be the problem most people are having. But, as we all know, a heart defect can go undiagnosed for a life time until its fatal effect brings it existence to the surface. Our problem, however, is that although that is the perceived cause of death, it's not the only one that has been put forward. This is simply why we're trying to find people who really knew her to see if there were manifestations of heart problems in the past."

"I can understand that, Mr Pollock. What I can't understand though is why you think that this young woman is Miss Andrea Colquhoun?"

"Pardon?" Both Pollock and Jacobstein stared at the clergyman.

"What makes you think the young woman is Andrea?"

"You were seen speaking to Miss Colquhoun outside the school gates at 4pm on the day she collapsed and died, sir. Another teacher saw you."

"Another teacher might have seen us talking, and I presume it was Mrs Jane Templeton as she certainly passed us on her way into the building, but it was not Miss Colquhoun I was talking to. A young teacher dropped a textbook as she came out of the gate, I happened to be passing and I picked it up for her. I presume she was a teacher but she certainly was not Miss Andrea Colquhoun." The silence that followed was deafening."

"You knew Miss Colquhoun well, I presume, Mr Carson?"

"Very well. I also know that she is, at this very minute, serving with the Jerusalem Missionary Society as a missionary in China. I see that this comes as a bit of a surprise to you gentlemen. Perhaps you would tell me exactly who identified the body?"

"The headteacher, sir." Pollock was finding it hard to understand it all, but in many ways that bombshell was beginning to make sense of the inexplicable. No items of a personal nature that would give a clue to their owner had been found and no real teaching experience seemed to come through. But what about the bookmark clue? Now Pollock realised that it and the poetry book probably had nothing to do with the Liverpool Irish. The unknown girl had somehow or other acquired them from Andrea Colquhoun along with the teaching certificates. But who was she?

"Would it be possible for me to see the body? Has no-one from Andrea's family been in contact?"

"Not yet, Mr Carson, which seems very odd."

"They are with the circus. Could be anywhere in Scotland or England. Wales, even."

"In that case, sir, we would be grateful if you would take a look. We'll send you over to the morgue by cab with one of my men. But right now I'd like you to answer a few questions on the Miss Colquhoun that you knew or know. If you are correct in what you've told us – no offence meant – then we must accept that there is some mystery here. An innocent one, though how someone impersonating another person can be that is beyond me. To impersonate someone as in this case either means that Miss Colquhoun has been robbed or is compliant in it."

"That latter suggestion is absurd!"

"More than likely, Mr Carson. But if you would just expand on the picture that we have of Miss Colquhoun at the moment. In all honesty, what we know about her is very little. She had all the relevant qualifications for teaching and as you've just told us, was very keen to do missionary work in China. That's about it, I'm afraid."

"Just falls short of less than nothing, Inspector Pollock. Ask away and I'll do my best to fill in that enormous gap."

"Thank you, sir. Can you tell me where she came from? I hope you don't object to DS Jacobstein taking notes?" Jacobstein gave the Reverend Carson his friendliest smile.

"Not at all As I said before, they're a circus family and so tend to move about with the seasons. The Colquhouns are originally from Belfast, Scotch Irish, but when the circus they were in came to Scotland, some of them stayed while the rest carried on. Their favourite spot was Bridge of Allan and after a very nasty accident, Andrea's grandparents settled there. That's where she grew up while her parents continued to perform. Still do, I believe. I've no doubt they'll read about this business in the newspapers at some point but maybe not for a while. It'll filter down, I'm sure."

"So her family are circus people?"

"That's right. Long tradition, she told me. Five of them in the act. Acrobats and trapeze artists. Her parents, two brothers and a sister, I think. The Colinotos. She said people who like the circus like Italian names. A bit of the exotic probably. There are other acts in the wider family but that's the name her immediate family use."

"Did you ever meet any of her friends?"

"A few of them. My wife has spoken to some of them at functions we have to raise money for the missions. Andrea was very keen to join our mission in China. We've several stations there. Her friends were all young people like herself. They were full of fun and very helpful with the baking and serving. The young men were always only too ready to lift heavy benches and the like."

"How long have you known her, Mr Carson?"

"About three years. My wife and I were serving with our mission hall in Paisley and she was living there. Andrea came to our services and my wife and Andrea got on very well."

"What was she like as a person?"

"My wife could answer that one better than I can but she always seemed very happy. She was very friendly, missed her family, though, I think. She was tutoring for private families, I believe. I don't know which schools, if any, she taught in. Don't know why I'm speaking in the past tense because I know she's actually in China." The three of them smiled ruefully.

"I take it she was trained for her future life in China?" Mr Carson nodded.

"Naturally. She's been training for the past two years. It's quite intensive and she was given a course in Chinese history, culture and languages. Dialects used where our stations are. Just to help them get by at the beginning but they're expected to develop that skill."

"And when did she leave for China?"

"Last September."

"And have you heard from her?"

"Not from any of the missions yet. It's too soon. We did get a letter from Hong Kong which Andrea posted when the ship called in there."

"Well, sir, it would seem that her credentials have been stolen."

"Oh dear. She might not even know it, Inspector Pollock, for she won't need any teaching ones at the mission. We run our own schools and Andrea wouldn't have been allowed to go if all things were not in order here. Do you think that young woman who died had stolen them?"

"That's possible, Mr Carson, we do know she certainly used them. Just one last thing," said Pollock as he lifted the manila envelope containing the bookmark that Quigley had placed on his desk, "does this mean anything to you?" Mr Carson smiled when he saw the bookmark.

"Where on earth did you find this?"

"It was found inside a book of WB Yeats' poems in the dead girl's lodgings. Do you recognise it?" said Pollock hopefully.

"I know this – perhaps not this exact copy – very well for my wife brought a dozen of them back from China when were posted back here. There are a million of these bookmarks circulating in China. This one might be one of those my wife gave away as small presents. Who knows?" The clergyman shrugged his shoulders. "There are probably another million circulating outside China, too. The Year of the Tiger is an especially popular one. It appeals to the rebel in all of us."

"I think that covers everything at the moment, sir, but perhaps if your wife thinks of anything that might help in our investigations, we would be most grateful if she would

contact us here in this police office. I take it that you've left your address with us, sir?"
"With the sergeant at the front desk."

The Reverend Alan Carson's exit was quickly followed by DC Austin Quigley's entrance, noisy and chaotic as ever, but always bearing the promise of something illuminating to come which seldom did. Perhaps it was his air of undiluted hope, perhaps the unconquerable optimism in his smile or, more likely, his comrades' longing to exit their own mood of despair.
"Sit down and get your breath back. I'll make you a cup of tea. Jake, you summarise what we've learned this morning both verbally and on paper." Quigey listened intently to the cultured tones of the DS.
"So," he said, "we're investigating the death of a young thief and impersonator?"
"Well," drawled Jacobstein, "I expect you could put it like that. Perhaps although the Far East angle seems incidental it could, in fact, be more important."
"Thank you, sir," said Quigley as he accepted his hot and strong cup of tea. Nobody could make it like the inspector, he thought. Learned that in the army, he reckoned. Austin Quigley loved being part of the CID team and his enthusiasm was both an inspiration to the other two at times although a cross to bear at others. Pollock resumed his seat.
"You're now up to date, Austin, but right now, Jake and I aren't. Spill it! I've got the bookmark you left when you came back. So, what did the revered Mr Smollett of JAE tell you about the bookmark, bearing in mind what we've already been told by the Reverend Alan Carson?" Quigley carefully placed his teacup minus saucer on top of a folded piece of thick paper and took out his notebook.
"Mr David Smollett is a real gentleman who knows everything there is to know about stationery. You should raise his salary, Jake."

"How many pencils did he sell you, Austin?" Pollock asked and managed to keep his face straight.

"None, sir, not one."

"Pens?"

"Two. I've already got a sufficiency of ink and I know how to make it."

"Now or before you met Mr Smollett?"

"Now."

"No notepads?"

"One – foolscap."

"He's right, Jake, Mr Smollett deserves a bonus for not selling Austin one of your pencils. That man has a soul and should thus be rewarded for it. Now, Austin, what did this paragon of stationery virtue actually tell you about the bookmark?"

"He recognised the bookmark straight off. Seems he collects them and he doesn't actually have that one. Chinese bookmarks are all very artistic and tasteful, he says, and much sought-after in the West. This one is especially treasured because of all the beautiful hand-embroidery throughout. Some have wonderful paintings on them but in that particular year, 1878-79, all the best were embroidered."

Both Pollock and Jacobstein whistled.

"Mr Carson said his wife had bought a dozen of the same when they were leaving their mission in China. Wonder if she ever became aware of their value in the West?"

"Probably not or it could have put paid to the fund-raising for a bit," Jacobstein suggested. Austin Quigley had more to say.

"They were only on sale in a very small region and were a limited collection. He said they had been made by a small, local commune. Mr Smollett also said that if the owner was thinking of selling it, he'd be more than happy to have a chance at making an offer."

"We'll keep that in mind, Austin. So now we know the history of the bookmark and how it was brought into this country, for it's a safe bet it was Mrs Carson who gave it to Andrea Colquhoun. We'll send someone round to ask her."

"We also know it was stolen by the dead girl. A guess but an educated one," Jacobstein added.

"Quite so, Jake, the original owner being Miss Colquhoun via Mrs Carson. Now Austin, the Rev Alan Carson is waiting downstairs for you to take him to see if he recognises the dead girl as Miss Colquhoun. Come straight back here after you've seen him into the cab that will take him home." Quigley smiled broadly. "Keeping the best to last, are we, Austin?" asked Pollock knowing exactly how Quigley's mind worked. Quigley nodded.

"Maybe, sir. Mr Smollett."

"Your stationery hero."

"Yes. He also said that the little commune had connections with Hong Kong and Scotland through the Army and unofficial marriages between soldiers and Chinese girls. And the people of the commune were also notorious agitators. They were not liked by the authorities, sir."

"Is that so? Well, you get over to the morgue with Mr Carson and we'll sit here and think that very interesting piece of information through." Quigley left at his usual speed.

"Now don't tell me, Ben, we're about to arrest Mrs Carson and Austin gets to write out the charge sheet with one his new pens?" laughed Jacobstein.

"Maybe it was a present, an innocent one, or maybe a meaningful gift from one rebel to another. I think we'll definitely eat in your store's famous restaurant at tea-time and I'll take great pleasure in watching your Uncle Avram give David Smollett what for for not selling Austin some pencils. This is just a sudden death, Jake, heart failure. Nothing suspicious except for that argumentative swine Jeffrey trying to rattle McPherson's cage. To sum it all up and correct me if I'm wrong, Jake, all Mr Smollett's information gets us nowhere."

"Can't say you're wrong, Ben. And we still know absolutely nothing about the dead girl. It's really tragic that a respectable young person liked by some, loathed by others, could just drop dead in a Glasgow street and be buried as an unknown, nobody to regret her passing, nobody to shed a tear."

"There might be some if only they knew. We're getting maudlin here, Jake. We'll write up our reports just now, take half an hour to think things through."

Twenty minutes were enough for Pollock to sit thinking.

"Let's try a different tack. Fancy a trip to the circus? Watch the Colinotos? Have a look in that newspaper over there and see where they're performing."

"Who's circus?" asked Jacobstein as he thumbed his way through the Daily Record. But that was as far as he got for Bill Manley appeared at the office door with a young man in tow.

"Someone to see you, Inspector Pollock. As our cells and interview rooms are full at the moment due to a disturbance in The Clay Pipe, I'm afraid it will have to be in here. Our front office is also teeming with friends, relatives and opponents of those locked up." Manley moved aside and ushered the man into the office. "Mr Edwin McMaster, this is Detective Inspector Pollock of the Criminal Investigation Department. Mr McMaster would like to speak to you about Mr Peter Yair." With that Manley once more returned to the fray downstairs.

Pollock rose and pulled a chair up to the desk for Mr McMaster. The man looked in his late twenties and was almost as well-dressed as Jacobstein. But he seemed very agitated and it took him a while to compose himself.

"Inspector Pollock, I've come to learn how much progress has been made in catching the people who did this most vicious attack on my friend, Peter Yair. He had absolutely no enemies in the world."

"Well, Mr McMaster, I'd like to express my astonishment and anger that such a vicious assault on your friend has taken place. But secondly, we're CID and actually have no part at all in the investigation. That falls to our uniformed colleagues."

"I know. It was that sergeant at the front desk I asked and he said their enquiries were continuing. I could see that he was very busy, so I asked if I could meet the CID man Peter had talked to and that was you."

"That's right, sir, but the case were making preliminary enquiries about really didn't involve Mr Yair."

"He said it did. That's what Peter told me. He was very upset."

"There was really no need for him to feel that way, Mr McMaster. We were at his lodging house to see a dead woman's room. He told you about her, I take it?"

"Yes, he did."

"We merely asked a few questions about the young woman and he knew very little but was as helpful as he could possibly be."

"That's not what he told me." Pollock had been in this aggressive situation many times before and knew that it was simply distress and anxiety that caused it.

"I've no idea what Mr Yair told you, sir, but I can assure you he was as helpful as he was able to be and we were very grateful. He was quite friendly and relaxed when we left."

"He said you forced him in a subtle way to tell you about Helen."

"Helen?"

"Yes, Helen. Remember her? She's lying dead in the morgue where you yourself probably sent her."

"That's Miss Andrea Colquhoun," said Pollock somewhat baffled.

"That's just the name she's living under to throw her husband off the scent." Pollock and Jacobstein were both stunned but only for a moment for Bill Manley entered without knocking, handed Pollock a note and left as quickly and silently as he had come. Pollock read it and passed it to Jacobstein. He turned back to McMaster.

"Have a seat, Mr McMaster. I'm afraid your friend Peter Yair is dead."

Pollock and Jacobstein sat alone in the make-shift office once more. Manley poked his head round the door as Jacobstein rustled the mewspaper.

"Which circus, Ben?" Jacobstein asked.

"The circus will have to wait, Ben, for you have a very irate lady waiting for you downstairs. We have one interview room free but everything's filling up fast so please don't dawdle." With that Manley vanished again.

"Have you realised , Jake," said Pollock, "that that's the only kind of lady we ever meet? Irate, aggressive, sarcastic, sardonic and that's it. If it wasn't for Shameena, I'd think that was how God made them. You've always got your Aunt Zena, I suppose. Here goes."

The irate lady almost flew at Pollock as he entered the very small interview room.

"Where is my daughter?" she screamed at him. Pollock reckoned his age made him the DI in her estimation.

"And who is your daughter, madam? What's her name and more immediately, what's yours?"

"You're Detective Inspector Pollock. Where is she?"

"I know who I am. What I'd like to know is your name and that of your daughter and until I receive that information, we will get nowhere."

"I'm Maggie Colquhoun and my daughter is Andrea. Now, where is she?"

"Your guess is as good as mine, Mrs Colquhoun."

"Don't tell me she's in the morgue for that's impossible."

"I quite agree with you, Mrs Colquhoun."

"What?"

"The young woman who is lying dead in the morgue has not been identified as yet. We do know that she is not who she was pretending to be, namely your daughter."

"And how do you know that?"

"The Reverend Alan Carson knows your daughter and he has been to the morgue and has sent word back that the body is not Miss Andrea Colquhoun."

"So why did you think it was her?"

"She had your daughter's teaching certificates and had been employed as a teacher here in Glasgow for some time under the name of Andrea Colquhoun. You can understand why we had no reason to suppose the dead teacher was not who she purported to be."

"So I've come through here for nothing? Missed an afternoon's performance for nothing?"

"Not exactly, Mrs Colquhoun. We'd like to know a little more about your daughter's personal life. That information might let us know a little more about how her possessions came to be stolen. There was also a poetry book we think belonged to her in her lodging house."

"I know nothing about her personal life. She always did as she pleased. She had a soldier for a boyfriend then gave him up when she discovered religion. Her true desire was to be a missionary in China. Now, I'm out of here. We're performing in Hamilton if you need me or her father." The very energetic lady paused. "And, Mr Policeman, Andrea thought poerty was a load of tripe." The door slammed with a bang and both Pollock and Jacobstein just stared at each other.

"Yeats has just been binned, Jake, and I'm for your restaurant right now. Come on! And between couses, try and figure out who Helen is?"

Chapter 4

Jake Jacobstein sat perusing the menu and ignoring his Uncle Avram's hostile glances. He took out his pocket-watch from his waistcoat pocket and knew exactly what the time would be. He had looked at it every five minutes since he had arrived. His hunger overcame all other feelings and he looked carefully this time at the menu card on the table before him.

"Fish and chips," he ordered, "for two." To his relief, he spotted Ben Pollock walking smartly onto the restaurant floor of Jacobstein's American Emporium. Uncle Avram vanished silently as Pollock approached his nephew's table. Pollock was a man with no time to wait for food and Uncle Avram admired any person dedicated to his work. Pollock sat down, glanced at the menu and then looked across the table at the DS.

"You ordered?"

"Two minutes ago." His boss did not ask exactly what had been ordered for him as it never changed.

"Bread and butter and tea, too?" Jacobstein nodded.

"It's all in." He also felt very hungry.

"I love this place, Jake, it was made for me." Pollock rubbed his hands together in anticipation. "Haddock and chips, the food of the gods."

"Ambrosia," corrected Jacobstein.

"Celtic gods, DS Jacobstein. They didn't mess about. Is there enough vinegar there, do you think?"

"Plenty. How did you get on at headquarters?" Pollck had received a summons from on high, as he put it, just as they had been leaving the police office.

"Depends on what you and I were hoping for, so, good and bad. Here's the fish and chips. Hello, Uncle Avram. I was just asking Jake here if he thought there was enough vinegar in the wee glass bottle."

"Depends on whether you want to drown the fish or savour the subtle flavours. DI Pollock, I'm here to serve so which one are you opting for?"
"You can't drown a dead fish, Uncle Avram, but I get your point. What's already here will be quite sufficient." Uncle Avran stood aside as the waitress served the food.
"Enjoy your meal, gentlemen," he said as the two CID men fell upon the food with gusto.

It was some time later, and having poured his sergeant a second cup of tea, when Pollock, a thick piece of buttered bread now in his hand, finally answered Jacobstein's question in full.
"The death of the young woman."
"Helen."
"Yes, Helen God Knows What has been placed officially on the back burner and we're, equally officially, now on the murder of Peter Yair."
"Good. But unofficially, Ben, do you think they might be one and the same case?"
"That is exactly my thoughts on the matter. We really don't lose one and gain another for we might just see Peter Yair's death as a massive step along the way to solving the first. Men and women are beaten to death in this huge city every day although that is seldom noted as the cause of death on the death certificate. That is a great blight on this city today. So, Jake, Peter Yair might just be another statistic bearing witness to a hobby of a certain type of manic citizen we harbour among our 800,000, but, then again, he might not. We've been charged with the task of bringing the murderers to book mainly because his second cousin's a town councillor. Amazing what constitutes a man with influence in this city today. Otherwise, it would have been put down as the result of a drunken brawl whether or not there had been witnesses or any evidence of drink having been involved."
"Uncle Avram was right about the vinegar, wasn't he?"

"As always. Have you noticed your uncle and I always have that same conversation whenever we eat here?" Jacobstein laughed and saw to the bill.

The dampness in the air hit them as they left the department store.

"We're in for rain," said Pollock turning up his collar against the cold. Jacobstein nodded and asked,

"Where to now?"

"Bosworth Street. The house has been broken into and trashed." Pollock's eyes spotted a tram and he began to run with Jacobstein at his side. They swung themselves onto it. It was a short ride along to the stop just before Bosworth Street. There seemed to be more spectators masquerading as pedestrians but no doubt the police presence there had caused that.

"Where did the assault take place, Ben?"

"In Lavender Street, oddly enough the same street that houses the Jerusalem Mission church"

"Any idea what he was doing there?"

"The report tells us nothing. Picked up on the street, taken to the Royal Infirmary and died there not long after we'd left. Identified by documents in his wallet which, incidentally, contained an envelope addressed to Peter Yair at his Bosworth Street address."

"So we must also speak to his friend Edwin McMaster?"

"As soon as possible, Jake. I'm sorry to run this investigation in tandem with the dead girl's one but there's a definite tie-up here, I can feel it. First of all, let's find out exactly who Peter Yair was and the best person to tell us that is the somewhat excitable McMaster. From him we should be able to discover the identity of Helen, our mysterious, deceased school teacher." Pollock started to walk down the street.

"The eternal triangle, Ben, in a manner of speaking," commented Jacobstein.

"Well, if it is, two sides of the triangle have collapsed never to rise again."

They eased their way through the small gathering outside the terraced house. From the murmurings, it was obvious that Yair's death had reached the neighbourhood. A constable saluted them at the gate and they soon found themselves inside the house they had left the previous day. Austin Quigley waved them into a small study just off the main entrance hall.

"You're at the coal-face so to speak, Austin, so tell us what's been happening and leave nothing out. Whoever trashed this place made a damned good job of it." Pictures, files and broken chairs littered the room and Pollock and Jacobstein had to wade through it warily to reach Quigley as he stood beside Yair's extremely sturdy desk.

"Made to last," said Jacobstein approvingly as he ran his fingers along the top.

"Not the drawers, though, I'm afraid, sir." Pollock agreed with Quigley as he picked up the shattered remains of one.

"God only knows what they clattered this with. It's like a jigsaw puzzle and there's the handle over there. A very angry and irritated person did this. Any contents remaining, Austin?" Quigley shook his head.

"Set fire to the lid." He pointed to the fireplace.

"Not much there," remarked Jacobstein. "I suppose the broken windows saw off the burnt smell."

"Looks like Yair cleared out his aunt's records and general correspondence when he first took over. He seems to have had an odd attitude to record-keeping. Wonder if he really was the nice man we spoke to yesterday, Jake?"

"I don't think so," replied the DS. "Know what this is?"

"What?" Jacobstein tossed the tiny object across to Pollock. Quigley moved to Pollock's side and they both peered at it.

"God in heaven! That's a very small part of a revolver. Now I wonder was it indeed Yair's or did it belong to the person or persons who trashed this house? Either way, I think it all will lead to the conclusion that Mr Yair led a very eventful and dangerous life. Could also, of course, mean that he was a simple gun salesman."

"As well as a chef? First-rate at making madeira cake?" Jacobson suggested. Pollock smiled faintly and said,

"Many a man has a hobby different by far from his regular job."

"Have you, sir?" asked Quigley with interest.

"No, Austin, I learned all about guns the hard way, in the army. I think if I had time to spare, I would spend it sitting by the fireside doing nothing." Jacobstein and Quigley exchanged sceptical glances. "Now, somebody has taken this place apart. They were looking for something specific. I wonder if they found it?"

"Were there any witnesses at all to Yair's assault? Even just a glimpse of it?" asked Jacobstein.

"None. He was lying in a lane just off Lavender Street. Passers-by probably thought he was drunk. We've no idea when it happened but it was probably during the previous evening the medical folk say. He was also quite possibly just dumped there. If it had happened here, the lodgers would have heard the commotion and raised the alarm. As it was, the lodgers were out when the wreckers came here and did their work – thoroughly. All this is according to this report." Pollock waved a few sheets of paper in the air. "Where are the lodgers now, Austin?"

"All in their rooms guarding their possessions except a Miss Columbine. She's in the sitting-room."

"Damnable that innocent folk should be put through this. Austin, you and a constable search all the rooms with a fine toothed comb. We'll see if the other paying guests can tell us anything at all either about odd happenings of late or anything at all about the late Peter Yair. And where the hell is Edwin McMaster? Bill Manley says he told him he was Yair's mate. If they were great friends then he probably visited here. That would explain how he came to know the unknown Helen but not why Peter Yair said he didn't."

Jake Jacobstein glanced quickly through the short list and groaned. Pollock looked at him, puzzled.

"Something wrong, Jake? Not the fish, was it?" Pollock's concern for his colleague's health knew no bounds as he had had the fish, too.

"Certainly not! It's one of the names on this list."

"There's one that gave me a bit of a jolt, too, Jake. Which one?"

"Maurice Hamilton."

"That's all right for it's Mr Snowball I'm looking forward to having a word with for I quite fancy knowing why a riveter from a Govan shipyard is now living in an establishment accurately designated genteel poverty. Why do I always associate genteel poverty with women, Jake?"

"Because hardly any men actually manage to live to that age. They mostly tend to go out with a bang long before they reach the equivalent of aged spinsters."

"Right, we'll see him first as he's first on the list and you might as well get whatever is embarrassing you over."

"Not really embarrassed, Ben, just that Maurice Hamilton might be. You see, he was the floor-walker in the gents' department in JAE for twenty years before he retired three years ago."

"So he knew young Joseph Jacobstein man and boy?" Jacobstein nodded and looked rather miserable. "Didn't catch you nicking a pair of gloves, did he?" Pollock was enjoying this. Jacobstein's sour look let Pollock know exactly what he thought of that one.

"It might just make things a bit awkward, that's all."

"Not if you both have clear consciences, it won't. Now, Austin, show in Mr Maurice Hamilton, please."

The best parlour was infested with upright chairs all crowded round a Dutch-tiled fireplace. Pollock placed a slender chair in front of the over-loaded mantle-piece and sat in front of it facing the empty chair. He waited. Jacobstein stood by the window and wished he were dead. Pollock suddenly rose and smiled his most beatific smile as Mr Maurice Hamilton appeared ushered in by DC Quigley. Hands were shaken, warrant cards shown and everyone except Quigley sat down. He exited at a slight nod from his boss to make sure the wily riveter did not scarper.

"Now, Mr Hamilton, our main aim in interviewing your good self is this." Hamilton finally looked away from Jacobstein and smiled broadly at Pollock.

"Our Mr Joseph's done well for himself in the CID, hasn't he, Inspector Pollock?" A source of pride was the young Jacobstein to the whole of the JAE workforce. Pollock had met it before.

"He's a credit to all of you who have had a hand in his development, sir. Now what I'd like to know is two-fold. Firstly, do you know anything at all of Mr Peter Yair's background? As you already know, this is now a murder enquiry." Mr Hamilton shook his head in anguish.

"Such a thing to have happened to a fine, upstanding young man, inspector. We live in very unpredictable times. Now, let me think. I'll just summarise, if you don't mind. It'll save you and Master Joseph, sorry, DS Jacobstein precious time. I've met Peter Yair on and off many times over the years since he was a boy. He was always cheery, open and pleasant. Worked in import-export, I believe. But that's only an impression for I never heard anything definite to back it up. Think he sponged a bit off his aunt, the lady who owned this place. He was related in a way to the Yairs of Selkirk, he once told me. They're an old Borders family with old money to go with it. How he ended up with very little, I don't know. Then again, maybe he still had it but preferred to live off other people. Not a nice trait, but his charm glossed that over. That's really all I know about his background except that at one time he worked for Jardine Matheson in Hong Kong."

"Did you know Miss Colquhoun, by any chance, Mr Hamilton? I got the impression from Mr Yair that she kept herself very much to herself."

"Just met her once in passing. She didn't seem the retiring type to me, in fact, she had a very aggressive way with her. Barged past me going out the front door as I was coming in. No apology and no thanks either when I helped pick up some correspondence she'd dropped. That's how I know who she was. Her name was on an envelope. Collie Pierot confirmed it for she was coming down the stairs. She said she knew her mother and that she was very aggressive, too."

"Just a moment, Maurice," said Jacobstein intervening, "we are actually talking about the girl who died suddenly in Society Street, aren't we?"

"Oh no, that's Helen, Helen Rowley. Peter Yair told me that she had collapsed and died. Miss Colquhoun never lived here." Pollock and Jacobstein stared at each other for a few seconds.

"Mr Hamilton," asked Pollock, "when did you collide with Andrea Colquhoun?"

"A week past last Tuesday."

"Do you know anything at all about Miss Rowley's background?"

"Sorry. Just smiled and said 'Good Morning' a few times. Nothing at all, really."

"It seems that Mr Yair was a good friend of a man called Mr Edwin McMaster. Do you happen to know anything at all about him? Where he lives? He called to see us but left when word came through that Mr Yair had died." Maurice Hamilton thought long and hard about this one.

"He's in the catering business. Has a café in the High Street. Married to an Italian lady, Gina Brossi. It's one of four Gina's family own. The family are old and valued customers of JAE. You remember young Enzo we took on as a messenger at weekends eight or nine years ago, Mr Joseph? He didn't last a day for we then discovered he couldn't ride a bicycle and had no intentions of learning?" Jacobstein nodded and laughed at the recollection of a message-boy who thought he could fit the job in with his penchant for just sallying round the area window-shopping. Well, Enzo," continued Hamilton, "is a scion of the Brossi family. A studying law last I heard and still can't ride a bicycle."

"So you would recommened a visit to the café, Mr Hamilton?"

"Take it from me, Inspector Pollock, it will be a very pleasant experience."

"Do you have any idea who will inherit this place now, Mr Hamilton?" But Hamilton shook his head and Pollock knew he would have to get on to that aspect very soon.

"None at all, I'm afraid. I'm simply a lodger and not privy to such information." With that, Pollock and Jacobstein parted company with JAE's former employee.

Jacobstein scribbled in his notebook and Pollock thought long and hard.

"We have Helen Rowley and Andrea Colquhoun with Peter Yair the link between them. Austin!" Pollock yelled and Quigley quickly entered. "Helen Rowley – see if we've got any information on her. She's the girl – I think – who was impersonating Andrea Colquhoun." Quigley left at speed as the DI turned towards Jacobstein. "That was a bit revealing, wasn't it? The real Andrea Colquhoun alive and well here in Glasgow within the last fortnight and the dead girl's name is Helen Rowley. And the Chinese connection yet again with Yair having lived and worked in Hong Kong. We might find out quite a lot from Edwin McMaster and get something good to eat at the same time. Whose next?"

"Your favourite lodger, Mr Cecil Snowball."

"Cecil Snowball, King of the Clydeside riveters and master safe-breaker. Neither titles are true for he lasted one day at the riveting and got five years for breaking into a safe but not actually managing to prise anything out of it." Pollock raised his voice, "Come in, Mr Snowball! It's been a while since we last met." Jacobstein was looking forward to his boss revealing in his questioning exactly where the two men had indeed last met. Pollock had a prodigious memory for names and occupations. Had he been in the team that had arrested Cecil Snowball? Jacobstein had to admit that Snowball's names were not easily forgotten.

"Nice to see you again, Mr Pollock," said Snowball taking the seat the inspector indicated. "You've come up in the world. I first met you when you were a detective constable and now look at you!" Snowball looked and sounded impressed and ever so slightly apprehensive. Pollock beamed back at his favourite riveter.

"And you've come along quite a bit yourself, Cecil. Outgrown your wife and five children, have you?" asked Pollock innocently, his benevolent look sitting easily on his face.

"I set them up for life and then hit the trail."

"Govan to Tollcross?" Snowball grinned and nodded.

"And a bit of gentility, too. Nice folk here, well, some of them. Mr Hamilton, for instance. A gentleman of the old school."

"Couldn't agree more. And now I suppose you'll tell me how you managed to set up your family for life, Cecil, although you have no need to tell me if you'd prefer not to."

"An uncle made it good in the goldfields of South Australia and happily died before he succeeded in squandering the lot. It's all well documented, Mr Pollock, nothing underhand about it. All the papers are lodged in the bank, his will and my receipt of the money. They've even got my will in their safe. I was his only living relative so the easy life beckoned. Then I discovered this nice, quiet boarding-house that suited me fine. Frequent visits to the racetrack are now affordable with some very moderate bets when I get there. Life is very sweet, sir. You an inspector, Mr Pollock? That's just the job. You'll agree, I'm sure, that I don't really ask much from life."

"I'm really pleased for you, Cecil. Now my own life would be just as sweet if you could provide me with some information." Mr Snowball sat upright and paid full attention.

"I'll do my best, Inspector Pollock. Now, what do you want to know?"

"Some background information on your landlord."

"Who is now a non-starter," finished Cecil Snowball.

"Quite so, Cecil. How long have you known him?"

"Not long. A rum lad, he was, and I know one when I see one. I've been casting my eye around for another billet."

Pollock was intrigued.

"Could you be a bit more specific, Cecil? A lot depends on what I can glean about him and his background bearing in mind this is a murder case."

"They say, gentlemen, that you're known by the company you keep. Well, Yair kept very dubious company. Not here but well away from this street."

"Example?"

"I was at Aintree in March. The Grand National. Put a bit on Father O'Flynn to win at 20/1 and the horse did just that. Funny how the old saying that money begets money seems to be true. Didn't win a lot because it's just a flutter I go in for these days, but the thrill of winning is just the same to me. Anyway, I saw Yair at Aintree. Not once did I see him place a bet but I did see him with a lot of different ladies."

"A ladies man, Cecil?"

"Oh no, sir, a pimp. Simple. He was one of those who hire out a better class of prostitute to men at big sporting occasions, but a cheap pimp just the same. That was what decided me on moving when he inherited this place. Bad enough when you don't actually know the girls involved, but when you do, it makes you sick to the stomach. You wonder what exactly is the hold he has over her for she's a really good young woman. Or was, I should say." Pollock and Jacobstein knew each was having the same thought.

"Her name?"

"Makes no difference now that she's dead. It was Miss Rowley, Helen Rowley. Not that type of girl at all, not financially down on her luck as most of these women are, and not that keen on Yair as a person judging by the way she acted when it was just the two of them. She came up with him from Liverpool and I made myself scarce on the same train."

"And now they're both dead, Cecil. What about his friend Mr McMaster? Ever meet him?" asked Pollock.

"Not actually met him, just overheard snatches of conversation. McMaster is an architect and was going to redesign this house as a teashop or café as he called it but intended retaining the top-floor as bedrooms. That's all I know. Maybe he was investing some money in the business. Sounded like it from the way he talked. Hope all this helps you out, Mr Pollock."

"Very much so, Cecil, and much appreciated. I'm really pleased that you received your inheritance and that you've taken care of the family." With that Pollock said 'Goodbye' and Mr Snowball left the room. The two CID men now had a lot to think about.

"Well, Ben, looks like old occupations as well as old habits die hard. Yair has come into some money and property here, but he still hankers after controlling women."

"And one woman in particular, Jake. I wonder if the late Peter Yair has a central role in our mystery?"

"And I wonder if he insisted on bringing her up with him from Liverpool?" Jacobstein chewed on his pencil.

"But what about the teaching position? She had to work hard there and what for? A complex man it seems he was, our Peter Yair," said Pollock thoughtfully.

"Do you think perhaps McMaster had invested in Yair's refurbishment plans and then saw his money going down the drain?" Pollock looked at his sergeant and shrugged.
"Who knows, Jake? That might make me go a bit hysterical, too, especially if it was the wife's money," he said.
"Or the wife's family's money," suggested Jacobstein.
"We'll need to sit down and discuss this. We'll do it when Austin reappears. Now, who is our final lodger? Sorry, this is genteel poverty, Jake, so resident is the expression."
"Our final resident, Detective Inspector Pollock, is Mrs Laeticia Pierot."
"Then wheel her in, Jake, and let's finish this part of the investigation."

Jacobstein duly wheeled the lady into the room in a cloud of the most enchanting perfume. Gardenia, thought Pollock, and old memories of foreign parts and exotic gardens were quickly squashed.
"Do sit down, Mrs Pierot."
"Columbine, Inspector Pollock, I'm Columbine Pierot."
"Really? How nice. I've got Laeticia Columbine Pierot written down here," said Pollock reading his notes once again.
"For official purposes only. As I know absolutely nothing of Mr Yair's doings or death, it's Columbine."
"As you wish, Mrs Pierot," Pollock said gently.
"And it's not Mrs, it's Miss," the rather attractive middle-aged lady informed him sweetly.
"I stand corrected yet again, Miss – is it Pierot?"
"No, inspector, it's Lambert, but Columbine Pierot will do. Please call me Columbine, just Columbine." Jake Jacobstein's face was perfectly straight and Pollock wondered how he managed it. Probably taught by Uncle Avram that the customer was always right and never, ever ridiculous.

"Just one or two questions, though, miss." 'Miss' gave him a very fetching smile. "We're investigating, as you obviously know, the death of your landlord, Peter Yair."

"A most revolting young man." That took the detectives by surprise.

"What makes you say that, Miss Pierot?"

"Too much charm. Never trust someone with too much charm. There's never anything behind it. Shallow. I'm an artiste in the music hall, Detective Inspector Pollock, and I see it all the time. Charm equals money. Turn it on, turn it off. I saw that with him and Andrea Colquhoun."

"Who?"

"Andrea Colquhoun."

"Are you saying you knew who she was when you saw them together?"

"Of course I did. I've known her since the day she was born. We're related, the Lamberts and the Colquhouns. Both circus families. My family are also trapeze artists but I injured my back and decided to train fox terriers for the theatre. My little family are looked after by Mr Pierot, a former clown. He stays with our dogs and I stay here. He gets up to whatever he gets up to and I do the same. Oh, nothing naughty, Mr Pollock, it's just that I like classical concerts and he likes the pub. We have a lovely life together – he's Pierot and I'm Columbine. That's our act's name." Pollock had to admit to himself that it sounded rather good.

"And what relationship do you think Peter Yair and Miss Colquhoun had, Mrs Pierot?"

"A very stormy one. Nothing emotional. Business, I woud say, but I don't know what kind of business."

"And when did you see them? Where? Here?" asked Pollock eagerly.

"I saw them here several times. I've seen the two of them twice since he took over from his aunt and that was in this house. Fighting like cats and dogs, they were, but keeping the noise down. The last time was about a week or so ago.

As far as I'm aware, they met in Hong Kong years ago – or so he told me anyway."

"And Miss Rowley?"

"I never even saw her far less met her. We worked different hours. I tend to stick to music halls near Glasgow so that I can have my independence, you know." She smiled indulgently at Jacobstein as he wrote in his notebook. "Young people are so keen to do well in their chosen profession, aren't they, Inspector Pollock? It's very touching." She suddenly addressed Jacobstein as a doting aunt would her favourite nephew. "And you're Mr Jacobstein from JAE," she commented softly. Jacobstein looked up and smiled. "You don't remember me, do you?" Mrs Pierot asked.

"If I'd met you before, Mrs Pierot, I'm sure I would remember." Pollock hoped the natural charm his sergeant was exhibiting was recognised as sincere.

"I was the lady who offered to give young Master McMaster bicycle riding lessons after that lad Enzo turned my offer down and Edwin McMaster was offered the job. Trick cycling was something most of us in the circus could do," she explained.

"I take it he refused?"

"A closed mind, Hasn't changed. Now don't let my fellow residents tell you it was all done and dusted with the refurbishment, gentlemen, you know, the relationship between Yair and McMaster, for it wasn't. It went deeper that just that. Would you hire a failed architect for your pet project? Yair was scum but he was no fool. Must be going, business calls." And with that, Mrs Columbine Pierot exited stage left.

Chapter 5

Jacobstein finished reading from his notebook, took a bite of his biscuit and then a long drink of his tea.

"That's about it, Ben. Did your search bring anything to light, Austin?" he asked his younger colleague.

"Not a single thing, Jake. Nothing out of the ordinary. Clean as a whistle."

"That's at least ticked that off our list," commemnted Pollock. "Now let's take each person we're interested in and see what we know and what we don't know. We'll begin with the first death, that of Miss Helen Rowley. Now, from what I heard, we learned a lot and nothing at the same time. I think we can safely say she did not have Liverpool connections however tenuous. She was seen in the company of Yair, the procurer of girls' bodies. Does that make her one of them? Who knows?"

"But they were none too friendly according to Mr Cecil Snowball," put in Jacobstein.

"You don't have to like the person you work for," said Quigley quite seriously.

"Are you complaining?" asked Pollock, eyeing his constable closely.

"Not at all," Quigley hastened to say.

"That's a relief," said Jacobstein flatly and Quigley knew he had a lot to learn when contributing to discussions.

"As DC Quigley says, there seemed to be no love lost between Helen Rowley and her employer, if indeed he was that. But, they were travelling together, there's no doubt about that."

"And he told us when we were in Bosworth Street that he'd barely met her. Merely a nodding acquaintance. Wonder if he recommended Bosworth Street to her when she was trying to give the husband the elbow? Before he inherited, that is? Quite the little liar, was Mr Peter Yair."

Jacobstein's expression showed clearly what he thought of the landlord and pimp.

"All charm and no substance, right enough. Right," said Pollock, "now back to Helen Rowley. We're only a little more enlightened. We still don't know anything substantial about her background or why she would take on the onerous task of posing as a teacher in an overcrowded classroom in Glasgow's East End."

"Could she have been a member of a particular political group, sir? She seems to have been on the side of the oppressed in her eyes."

"Good point, Austin. We'll ask a few questions about that. Do you fancy getting in touch with the lads who work on these groups once we're finished here?"

"I will, sir. I'd love to." Austin Quigley felt he was now beginning to move a little in his career. To be involved, even just asking them a few questions with the really serious movers in the world of policing was a huge feather in his cap at this stage in the game.

"Either heart disease in the family or Dr Jeffrey's picked a winner. Anything we've missed out?" asked Pollock as he checked his watch. "After this, I'm for home and bed. We'll see McMaster first thing in the morning, Jake, and Austin, you get in touch with the political men and dig deep. A lot might depend on what you find out from them. Now, I think that's about it with Miss Rowley. The poetry book could belong to anybody but my money's still on Andrea Coquhoun despite what her mother says. So, let's take the missing Miss Colquhoun first. Jake?"

"A school-teacher, family a circus act, had her teaching credentials used by another woman with or without her knowledge. We simply do not know. She might be the owner of a book of poetry that has a Chinese bookmark inside. We know she owned the bookmark but we're not absolutely certain that the book is hers. The book was left behind in the boarding-house."

"And we only have Peter Yair's word it belonged to the girl who had been using Helen Rowley's credentials. The book belonged to one or other of these two girls. Miss Colquhoun was definitely last seen in the boarding-house just over a week ago when she was supposed to be doing missionary work in China."

"And that, gentlemen, just about sums it up, I think," said Pollock, "except for the fact that when last seen, she was speaking to Peter Yair in his house and came away looking none too pleased. The question is, where is she now?"

"And why isn't she in China?" asked Jacobstein.

"After we've decided which are the main questions to be answered concerning our main players, we'll then decide how to go about finding the answers. Anything else on the elusive Andrea?"

"Can't think of anything right now, sir," said Quigley, desperate to get on and meet the men working on the underground movements.

"What about how she's earning her living since she's obviously not teaching," said Jacbstein. "The circus? Her folks are performing in Hamilton but could she be in a different circus or maybe a music hall act like Miss Columbine?"

"We'll follow that one up, Joe. She's around here somewhere and mad enough with at least Yair to pay no attention to whether the Reverend Alan Carson or any of his flock sees her. That alone should make her quite careless. I wonder if she knows all about Helen Rowley? Wonder if she was colluding with her in the teaching swap business. You know, this is a right fankle. All right, let's move on. Next up?" asked Pollock.

"I wonder why Helen Rowley was posing as a teacher? Why not try for a job as a shop assistant or a cleaning one? Why impersonate Andrea Colquhoun? Was there something between those two? Did Andrea Colquhoun suggest it? And why? Were these two girls sharing that room since the aunt died?" Jake Jacobstein shook his head knowing he had just asked questions they might never even get near to answering.

"We'll move on to the next in line for those girls are certainly very problematic," Pollock decided. "Peter Yair, the man of the moment. What do we know about him apart from the fact that he was beaten to death? It might, of course, turn out to be a serious assault that was just overdone in the heat of the moment."

"That doesn't get my vote, Ben," cut in Jacobstein and his younger colleague nodded in agreement before he spoke.

"It seems to me, sir, he was a shady character who was mixed up in at least one very unsavoury business. And, remember, he was an habitual liar."

"And that," said Pollock with a grimace, "is Peter Yair's obituary. A liar and a procurer of women. I think he would have preferred that more up-market term. But he did speak to us about his plans for converting the boarding-house and that seems to have been true albeit, as Miss Columbine pointed out, he'd hired a failed architect to do it."

"Maybe Yair was just hard-up," Quigley suggested thoughtfully.

"Not according to the lady. He'd inherited all his aunt's wealth a few months previously and he seems to me to be more into acquiring cash than spending it. His charm could have been responsible for attracting the ladies but only those of the younger generation. Mrs Pierot has been round the block a bit and fulsome, flattering phrases are like windows to her – easily seen through. I'll tell you this, I'd take her assessment of any man, any day. Now, I think that leaves us only to give a thought or two to the hysterical Mr Miles McMaster. Any thoughts on him?" Pollock shook the teapot and Austin took the hint and within five minutes, tea, biscuits and a long-forgotten box of shortbread all managed to lift the atmosphere a good deal. Pollock wagged a piece of that delicacy towards Quigley.

"When you meet those political johnnies tomorrow, Austin, don't make the tea. The meeting will take place in their office, not here where the jobs are shared. That is to say, son, you make the tea, Jake washes up and I get out the biscuit tin. Sometimes we swap jobs but it's all even. If we're too busy talking and the like, then Mrs Sleigh the cleaner does it and I leave her a few bob. We're CID, the three of us. We're given a case, watch the suspects we identify as in need of serious surveillance and then pounce. The politicos get a case, watch their suspects for years but seldom pounce. They've a geat deal of money and energy knocking about as they very seldom ever bother to move out of a restaurant. Let them make their own tea."

"Well, Ben, the obvious one is who killed Peter Yair, intentionally or otherwise? Is it in fact murder?"

"The powers that be, urged on by his well-connected relatives, say that it is. I'm wondering how much Miles McMaster knew about it? Did he know it was when he came to Camlachie police office and did he think he might be next?" The other two detectives were silent as Ben Pollock spoke.

"His hysteria would certainly lead me to suspect that, Ben. He could easily have been distressed at his client being badly hurt, but it was more than that. He was definitely scared out of his wits."

"As has already been suggested, Jake, maybe he was either on the verge of losing money he'd invested in the project or perhaps it was simply the loss of a good fee he couldn't withstand. It seems to me, we have a few possible eternal triangles in this case. We've got Helen Rowley, Andrea Colquhoun and Peter Yair on the one hand and Peter Yair, Helen Rowley and Miles McMaster on the other."

"Peter Yair and Helen Rowley connecting the two triangles, Ben."

"That they do, Jake."

"So where does the Chinese connection enter into it?" asked Quigley. Pollock shrugged slightly.
"Maybe not at all, Austin. But I suspect if you ask the right questions tomorrow, maybe mentioning Hong Kong and Yair's name in particular, we might just find out. Also give them the name of the missionary society written down on that piece of scrap paper there in front of you, and see if it rings any bells. Now, time to consider Mr Miles McMaster. No need to go over what we've just said about his possible involvement with Yair on business matters, the ones above board that is. Jake?"
"He's married to Gina Brossi, a daughter of Enzo Brossi who owns half-a-dozen cafes and ice-cream shops in Glasgow. He's reputed to be an architect but rumour from Miss Columbine says that he's not a very good one. We should maybe investigate that." Jake's notebook was a treasure trove of information half-forgotten by other less conscientious officers in the heat of interrogation. "He has a tendency to over-react but he left before we could delve deeper into it. He obviously knew Helen Rowley. That's about it, Ben."
"And that should do for today. We'll all meet here tomorrow at 8.30am and quickly flesh out the questions and also see if anything of note has come into our minds that we've missed out here." With that they went their separate ways.

Enzo's ice-cream shop cum café was quiet as Pollock and Jacobstein stood at the foot of the High Street and admired the sheer, overwhelming cleanliness of the shop-front sited diagonally opposite them. Red, white and green tiles decorated the outside of the café, a tantalising array of pastries drew admiring looks from all passers-by.
"Coffee and pastries, I think, Jake. Looks to me like we're in for a very depressing, rainy day. Somehow ice-cream and a soaking drizzle don't go together." They both looked up at

the grey sky that was growing more depressingly blacker with every passing minute. Jacobstein nodded his agreement.

"I wonder why we were told we could find Miles McMaster here? Doesn't he have an office of his own? Or doesn't he work for a firm of architects?"

"Or maybe he was just let out of Barlinnie jail a few months ago and is trying to find a way back into his profession," Pollock suggested as they stood and watched the comings and goings in the café.

"Barlinnie?"

"Now, now, DS Jacobstein, you don't think your esteemed leader went home last night and simply slept the sleep of the just, do you? A few chats with a few old-timers in The Clay Pipe put me wise to that. He got done for affray and police assault and lost his job as a result. He was actually dead drunk at the time. He had the great misfortune to run up against the only tea-total sheriff in Lanarkshire so his fate was sealed from the off. Hence he's helping out the in-laws in that branch of the Brossi empire. Maybe the Bosworth Street job was his first since freedom beckoned. It seems he's not one of Mother Nature's blessed ones. I think we should enjoy our coffee and cake before we introduce ourselves. You just never know when an unsolicited piece of information falls upon our ears from innocent people who have themselves absolutely nothing to hide." They let the traffic pass before venturing across the High Street.

The two detectives had just got settled when the rain came down like stair-rods and the High Street emptied and the café filled.

"Now, gentlemen, what would you like?" A small version of everybody's granny stood smiling by their green checkered, oilcloth-covered table, pencil and notebook in hand. "I'm Carla Brossi, Enzo's wife."

"Two milky coffees, please, and two cakes. Make them two of your best sellers, if you don't mind, as we're strictly shortbread and madeira cake specialists ourselves. We've decided to take life by the ears and go completely mad."

"I'll surprise you then?" said the lady trying not to smile. "So then, it's two of the not-quite-the-most-expensive-ones-but-near-enough?" Pollock and Jacobstein nodded in anticipation as the lady hurried off and both CID men relaxed. If Miles McMaster were inside the café, he would have exited fast if he had anything to hide. A bit of friendliness went a long way, Pollock had found, and he had decided to play that card that day. Besides, Jacobstein's standards as regards eating places was high and this particular one seemed to have pleased him immediately. His expression was invariably either half-hidden distaste or pleasantly pleased. That morning, he seemed exceedingly taken with Enzo's.

"Ever been here before, Jake?"

"No, but I think I'll definitely be here again."

"You will be if McMaster has done a bunk." Jacobstein sighed long and long-sufferingly.

"I mean as a paying customer, Ben."

"Can't say that for myself as I don't see fish and chips on the menu. I might be persuaded, though, if the cakes are top-rated."

The coffee and cakes were indeed top-rated and Pollock wondered which lucky lady would be taken there by Jacobstein. He finally decided that a meal at JAE's restaurant was more his own style but maybe Shameena would enjoy the ice-cream. He paid the bill and gazed about him as Enzo's wife handed him his change.

"May I have a quiet word with you, Mrs Brossi, in private, please?" he added as both men discreetly showed her their warrant cards.

"Certainly." Carla Brossi showed no surprise at all and led them through to a small office at the back of the café. Pollock wondered if the police were frequent visitors there or that life in the City Centre had inured her to all would-be surprises concerning the authorities. Once inside the office, they were introduced to Enzo himself who seemed more concerned with his arrangements for the Charity Cup Final than what the CID might want with his café.

"Have a seat, gentlemen. Can't think why you're here. Have you made any complaints to the police lately, Carla?" he asked. His wife shook her head, smoothed down her pristine white apron and made for the door. She stopped momentarily when she reached it and answered,

"None at all and especially nothing that would concern the CID. But customers are waiting and I'm sure that Enzo can help you. If you're really desperate, you'll find me serving our customers." With that, Mrs Brossi left closing the door firmly behind her.

"We would really like to speak to Mr Miles McMaster, Mr Brossi," said Pollock. "He was asking the other day about how our enquiries were going into the assault on his friend Mr Peter Yair. Word came in while he was there about the case becoming a murder enquiry. What my colleague and I are doing at the moment is trying to buid up a more complete picture of Mr Yair's background, his social life, business dealings and the like. We're interviewing his friends and associates, just trying to pull it all together. It could, of course, also have been a purely random attack. We've now reached Mr McMaster on our list and hoped to have a few words with him. In this kind of enquiry, time is of the essence and we're hoping to work through our list in the shortest possible time while still being completely thorough in our investigations. It then lets us move on to the next stage in our quest for a solution. Is Mr McMaster available, Mr Brossi?" Pollock sat back and hoped for the best.

"He certainly is. At this very moment, he's checking new deliveries in our storeroom. Not his usual job but he was here when it was delivered and offered to help. He's very particular so the right man for the job as my son is doing deliveries of our home-baked pastries right now. We supply certain high-class stores with them, you know." His pride shone through all right and why not, thought Jacobstein, switching to his entrepreneurial persona. "I'll call him."

Miles McMaster sauntered in as Enzo left and looked the epitome of casualness. He was cool, calm and collected and the detectives had difficulty recognising him as the man whose hysterics had overwhelmed him in their own office. He sat down behind Enzo's desk and waited without saying a thing. Whatever had brought the hysterics on had obviously now been fixed and Pollock knew that making any headway towards anything resembling the truth was going to be very difficult indeed, if not impossible. He gave Jacobstein a subtle nod.

"Good morning, Mr McMaster," said Pollock's sergeant, "our warrant cards, sir, although we all have recently met." McMaster made a show, a very measured show, of examining the cards. The man then sat back and placed his hands behind his head, hands clasped together.

"Well, gentlemen, what do you think of our café? Have you had something to drink? Would you like something to drink? No?"

"We've already sampled your coffee and cakes, sir," said Jacobstein, "and I for one will certainly be returning under less formal circumstances."

"Formal?" repeated McMaster smiling.

"All interviews when connected with a murder enquiry are formal although, as you are probably aware, not in a legal sense. We could call this particular one informal but it also means that we can officially record that we have interviewed you concerning Mr Yair's death, as indeed the same applies to all other friends and acquaintances of the deceased."

"What is it that you would like to know, Detective Sergeant Jacobstein? I'm more than anxious to see whoever was responsible for that outrage brought to justice."

"As are we, sir. At the moment, we are trying to establish Mr Yair's background. That is why we're talking to his friends, family and the residents of his boarding-house. Can you tell us, Mr McMaster, how long you have known him?"
McMaster smiled broadly at both detectives, then leaned forward resting his elbows on the desk.
"Let me think." He made a pretence of giving the matter great thought while Pollock gazed at the ceiling, noted the total lack of cobwebs and was suitably impressed. Jacobstein did his best to look like he was taken in by the theatricals.
"Anything come to light, sir?" he asked quietly and put McMaster down as a complete fool in his mental notebook.
"Yes indeed, Sergeant Jacobstein, it has. I now recollect that I really can't recall anything."
"So you can't remember when you first met Peter Yair?"
"No, I don't, for you see we were both only a few weeks old at the time. But I'm only surmising. I could give you my old nanny's name as she will probably remember for she has a remarkable memory for such occasions. You see, gentlemen, Peter was my cousin." Pollock stopped his cobweb watch.
"Really?" Jacobstein's surprise was genuine.
"Yes, indeed, so now you know why my concern was so profound."
"You have our deepest sympathy, Mr McMaster, for your cousin's death," said Jacobstein.
"You certainly do, Mr McMaster," added Pollock.
"Thank you. Now, before you ask me, yes, I know who his heir is. I am. I hope you don't think that automatically makes me the killer?" Pollock failed to raise a surprised and slightly outraged grin, Jacobstein did not.
"Not at all, Mr McMaster, for it would be a bit too obvious in this case. Would your close blood relationship be responsible for his hiring you as the architect for the plans for his new tea-rooms given your lack of recent success in

convincing your professional body of your trustworthiness" Fury leapt into McMaster's eyes but died again equally quickly. Pollock sat, his face blank, as he had known what Jacobstein was up to.

"Could have been, Mr Jacobstein, as family members can be extremely generous." The confident half-smile was attempted but failed miserably. Jacobstein continued relentlessly.

"Do you know how your cousin, Mr Yair, actually earned his living?" McMaster shrugged.

"Anybody's guess. Sponging off other family members, I suppose. That had always been a way of life with him. Did it very successfully, too." There was a slight note of envy in his voice. Maybe all that separated these two were one had charm in buckets, the other's bucket was empty, thought Pollock.

"Did Mr Yair gamble, do you know? Horses, perhaps?" asked Jacobstein.

"He had no interest in that direction that I know of, but I was not always in touch with him. Peter got in touch with me when he inherited the house and the money. He asked me to come up with some plans and drawings for converting the house."

"Had you yourself invested any money in the venture?"

"Yes, Sergeant Jacobstein, I had. Quite a bit, actually." And where did you get that, wondered Pollock. Now he knew why the assault had worried the shit out of the weasel in front of them. At least they now knew that McMaster was in the clear for trying to murder his cousin. Then a thought struck him. Maybe Yair's own debts would have swallowed up any money including the value of the house that he stood to inherit and McMaster knew that.

"And will you continue with Mr Yair's plans, Mr McMaster?" asked Pollock.

"Definitely not. That house will be up for sale as soon as possible." And any borrowed money from Enzo's under the counter so to speak, quietly replaced, thought the inspector.

"I'll probably invest it in the café business. A very nice little earner."

"Pleasant stroke of luck for you." Jacobstein smiled as he made that remark. McMaster's look of amiability dropped and was replaced by a menacing scowl that would have struck fear into most men but Jake Jacobstein had seen worse scum do it better.

"Did you know your cousin was a pimp?" That sudden question hit McMaster hard.

"I did not, sergeant, and you're a liar. Where's your proof? Peter was many things but not that. He had his pride in his well-respected family name, revered it's been for generations in The Borders. Why would he sully it in that despicable form? He had his faults but."

"Such as?" asked Pollock leaning in towards the desk and staring McMaster straight in the eye. But McMaster had shut up like a clam.

"Of course, sir," said Jacobstein, "there's really no need for you to feel upset. We all have various family members who sail close to the wind sometimes. If I could just finish by asking you one or two more questions along a different line and then we must be going." McMaster made to stand and close the interview.

"Sit down, sir, or we'll conclude this interview in Camlachie police office." Pollock continued to stare at the man as he spoke. "I suspect that wouldn't go down too well with the in-laws. The partnership with the Brossi family might come a cropper like the Yair one did."

"You're a pair of despicable bastards," shouted McMaster, slumping back into his chair again.

"No need to raise your voice, sir, and we're not really. It's just that some really despicable bastards bring out the worst in us. Now answer all, and I really do mean all, of Detective Sergeant Jacobstein's question truthfully." The menacing scowl that Pollock gave McMaster very nearly scared the shit out of his sergeant. It did that to McMaster but Jacobstein was too well brought up to comment and Pollock had smelled it all before. "Your time might mean money but our time could mean life or death for someone, and believe me, Mr McMaster, that someone will not escape us." Jacobstein launched right in.

"Helen Rowley. Exactly when and how did you know her and forget the cradle talk! You didn't meet her when your knickers were full of shite."

"About three years ago. I met her in Hong Kong." McMaster had seen the light.

"What were you doing there?" asked Jacobstein trying hard to mask his profound interest with one simple question.

"Working, I was working. Peter and I worked for Jardine Matheson."

"And what was Helen Rowley doing there?"

"She was there with her husband."

"Did he also work for Jardine Matheson?"

"No, he was attached to the regiment stationed there and she lived in the married quarters."

"Were you surprised to find her living in Yair's boarding-house?"

"No, Peter said he'd recommended it to Helen before he inherited it. She and I never spoke except for the occasional 'Good day!'. That's it. That's the truth. There was no need to renew a friendship that had never existed and she was very basically working-class."

"So she worked and you didn't because you'd been barred from your profession? I can see what you mean." Jacobstein was now in full flow but Pollock stepped in.

"Her husbad's name, if you please, Mr McMaster."

"Nigel Rowley, Sergeant Nigel Rowley. He was a friend of Peter's, not mine."

"Peter Yair was the classless type, was he?" McMaster tried the scowl again with the same amount of success.

"Not so much classless as tasteless. Everyone was fair game to Peter. He was truly one of your despicable bastards."

"Do you know something, Mr McMaster," said Pollock rising, "I think I'll buy some of Carla's cakes and take them back to the office in Camlachie. Thanks for your co-operation." With that, Pollock and Jacobstein left the office. Miles McMaster waited a while then hurried off to a fatal rendezvous. The decision had been made and the sooner the deed was done, the better.

Chapter 6

The three CID men sat back in their office in Camlachie, thoroughly satisfied with the labours of whoever Enzo hired as a pastry cook.

"Delicious! Excellent! Nearly as good as a hot jam turnover from Dough Frae Me's," said Pollock, smacking his lips and checking to see if there was another cupful in the teapot. He was out of luck. "So, gentlemen, our next step is an odd one, I think. At least it's once more moving away from Peter Yair's murder to concentrate yet again on Helen Rowley. We think they're definitely linked but our superior officers might differ. I'm told that our superintendent has toothache so we might as well strike while the iron's hot and take this case in whatever direction we want to. We think that the three of them, Yair, Colquhoun and Sergeant Rowley were in Hong Kong at the same time. We now have a fourth name, that of Mr Miles McMaster, at best a total creep, at worst a slippery wee swine. We also know that McMaster is sitting pretty because he's now, we assume, debt-free as he is Yair's heir."

"A good reason to kill him if things were becoming really desperate for McMaster," said Quigley.

"Seems a hapless type, though, Ben. Came across as a bit short on grit. Weak is probably the best word I can think of to describe him." Pollock nodded in agreement.

"Seems that way, doesn't it? Then again, he could be working with someone."

"But who?" asked Jacobstein.

"Well, let's look at the four of them plus Rowley's wife, Helen. Let's look at what we think might have been their lives in Hong Kong," said the inspector. Jacobstein was first to come up with a suggestion.

"Ex-pats, colonial types?"

"One of them was a soldier, though."

"Depends on how much free-time, he had. Maybe Helen wanted to socialise with them in preference to the wives of the other ranks." But Austin Quigley shook his head.

"But, sir, you have already said she was on the side of the workers." Pollock smiled, impressed.

"You're right, Austin," he said, " for going up in the world seemed to mean taking the entire working-class with her." Jacobstein was not convinced.

"That didn't necessarily mean Rowley herself was above socialising with the others," he remarked seriously.

"Certainly McMaster and Yair would be very junior members of Jardine Matheson regardless of their family connections and Andrea Colquhoun was a circus performer by profession. There are all levels of social groups. It just depends on the group's main interest," said Pollock frowning. "So, gentlemen, how do we find out what that was in the quickest possible time? McMaster's a washout. He's totally concentrating on his inheritance. Thinks he's home and dry so will simply clam-up."

"Ask Sergeant Rowley," suggested Jacobstein.

"And Miss Colquhoun," added Quigley.

"If we can find her, Austin, certainly. Now, you said that the big boys have nothing on Helen Rowley."

"Absolutely nothing."

"According to them?"

"According to them. I thought they'd be oozing power but they were quite quiet-spoken and matter-of-fact." Quigley was unimpressed. Pollock and Jacobstein exchanged amused glances.

"Everybody's favourite uncles. Wouldn't swat a fly. That's them alright, isn't it Jake?"

"Sweeties on Fridays and presents at Christmas. Too good for this world." Jacobstein's head was firmly in his notebook, his grin unnoticed by the would-be high-flier.

"Maybe thinking of sticking with the CID after all then, son?" Pollock suggested, making a half-hearted attempt to hide his amusement. Quigley had begun to look extremely uncomfortable as it dawned on him he would never be allowed to forget his fleeting notion of jumping ship. "I think the first thing for us to do is to interview Sergeant Rowley who has been tracked down to Maryhill Barracks. As the lady's name has appeared in the newspapers as Miss Colquhoun, he's had no need to contact us. Austin, you'll come with me, see how the real high-powered men work, and Jake, will you have a go at eliciting some details of how the foursome met and what they got up to. And Austin, watch how Jake and I do all this without recourse to Friday sweeties and Christmas presents. Find out, Jake, if Helen Rowley was also one of the set. Give McMaster a real going-over this time. Working at it from your end and ours will perhaps bring something hidden to the surface. The sergeant's answers might differ from McMaster's. We'll take a cab and drop you off at the High Street. Come back here when you've finished and we'll take stock before planning our next move. And you, Quigley, keep your mind off the Cup Final on Saturday and on the job. I had a bit to do with the Secret Service boys in India and believe me, son, that crowd were at no point up against it as much as the police in this city will be on Saturday night. Get your admiration pointing in the right direction. This is where the real action is." Jacobstein nodded solemnly in agreement. "Right, folks, let's go. I've got the distinct feeling we'll get nowhere with Mrs Colquhoun and the Colinotos, so maybe we'll tackle Miss Columbine instead. What the hell are we supposed to call that woman? Anyway, speaking to her is for later." Pollock was still asking if it was Mrs Lambert or Miss Pierot or what as he raced down the stairs.

Pollock watched as Jake Jacobstein closed the cab door and then vanished among the crowds thronging the High Street. The cab then carried on and finally entered Maryhill Road, the vast military baracks looming up on their right. Pollock paid the cabbie and, with Quigley by his side, strode like the ex-sergeant he was, up to the control post. Oddly enough, although born and bred in Glasgow, he had never been inside these barracks during his long years of service.

It was sometime before Sergeant Rowley appeared in the small office Pollock had been assigned where he could interview and break the bad news of his wife's death to the soldier. He wondered if the man already knew, wondered if either Yair or McMaster had known it all and had informed Rowley. He shook hands with him and the three of them sat down. Pollock lost no time in breaking the sad tidings. Rowley looked stunned, his face paled dramatically against the dark colour of his uniform, and Pollock waited until he had recovered.

"Your wife wasn't wearing a wedding ring, Sergeant Rowley and, at first, we were led to believe she was someone else. Now, would you mind answering a few questions for us, sir?"

"I don't mind at all, if it will help." Rowley answered more automatically than anything else as his thoughts seemed miles away. He suddenly looked straight at Pollock and said, "Why did you think that she was somebody else? Who?" He was sincerely just as puzzled by it all as were the detectives in front of him.

"Before I answer that, sir, can you tell me how long you've been in either Glasgow or indeed Scotland?"

"How did Helen die? And why are you, the CID, involved?" Pollock decided there and then that he would leave no stone unturned, that he would get right to the bottom of this whole stinking affair.

"I think, Sergeant Rowley, that we should take this in a very ordered manner with me asking the questions. You can then feel free to ask me as many as you think fit." Rowley did not look any too pleased at being told what to do. He was a sergeant in one of the finest regiments and was used to giving orders to those of lower ranks. Pollock and Quigley in their cheap suits were certainly not of the ruling classes above him. Just for a moment, Pollock wished he had brought Jacobstein along with him for he reeked of class and his clothes discreetly yelled money and taste. Still, Pollock knew he had his own method of establishing who was in charge. "I met a few of your fellow soldiers when I was serving in India and I'm telling you, we sergeants had one hell of a party that night." Rowley laughed and relaxed.

"You'd think we'd be used to death but that's not the case. Ask away, DI Pollock, for I've nothing to hide and neither had my wife."

"Excellent, Sergeant Rowley. To explain our involvement in your wife's death, it's really only because there is some dubiety about the cause of death. There is a slight question mark over it simply because one expert is not wholly satisfied. We've been asked to look at the circumstances surrounding the death and report back to our superiors."

"There's a disagreement then over the the cause of death and you're examining the facts? Does one of the experts think then that it is a murder case?" asked Rowley sharply.

"The possibility of that does exist at the moment. As I've said, we have no absolute proof of any irregular behaviour, so this is definitely not a murder enquiry as yet. It stands every chance of being a very unfortunate but natural death. I'll make my report and my superiors will decide what will happen next. Unfortunately, we've discovered a tenuous connection between your wife and another case we're investigating, so we need to establish whether or not that is purely coincidental. That is the reason we're here now. We have not approached you before as her next-of-kin because Mrs Rowley was known under a different name."

"That's ridiculous!"

"You find it ridiculous, Sergeant, but we find it not uncommon in a city of some eight hundred thousand souls. Your wife was not living in married quarters, sergeant, so could you please explain that to us. We have no interest in your private life as such, but this could have made Mrs Rowley more vulnerable." Quigley kept his head well-down over his notebook. Rowley looked the fiery type and there was no way he wanted a broken jaw. He was going to that cup final and not to any infirmary. Pollock had dealt with Rowley's type a hundred times before and knew how to cope with it, but Quigley was sure that an innocent glance at Rowley by himself would easily rile the soldier and that jaw would go.

"We split up. Wasn't that unusual for us. It had happened before but we always got back together. Helen was a woman of great spirit, she loathed any kind of hierarchy – her words. Some soldier's wife, eh?" Rowley's expression was a mixture of amusement and regret. "Helen needed freedom and I didn't make any effort to stop her having it. I didn't know she was in the city. She didn't contact, me. I expect she meant to – eventually," he added, "before the regiment left. She'd know exactly what the regiment's movements were from her friends, the other wives, you know. But I'd really like to know how she died before we go any farther and what the experts disagreed on, Inspector Pollock."

"Your wife collapsed suddenly in Society Street in the East End and the death was recorded by the police surgeon and later the pathologist as heart failure. The pathologist, though, suspected a drug overdose although he had no definite proof of this, just a strong suspicion, so we were asked to take some time off from our current duties to pursue the circumstances surrounding the death of your wife. At the moment, the official cause of death is still heart failure. I can tell you no more as there is no actual evidence, solid evidence, of wrong-doing. Young people have been known to pass away suddenly in this fashion." Rowley was obviously perplexed.

"What drug? Helen was very strict in not taking, or even giving to me, any drug that had not been prescribed."

"Well, Sergeant Rowley, I'll come to that directly. Now, you said that you and your wife were unofficially separated." Pollock nodded in agreement.

"We were apart but just for the time being. Helen was my wife and I wanted to keep it that way."

"And when did this parting take place?" asked Pollock.

"About six months ago roughly."

"And when was the last time you spoke to her?"

"When we parted that day. It was nothing formal. In some café or other and I just thought she intended going back to her grandparents as usual in Liverpool. I didn't give it any more thought. I had no idea she was living in Glasgow."

Pollock wondered why Rowley had not asked more about the other woman they had thought her to be.

"Had Mrs Rowley ever been involved with the police?" He had had to ask that and he now waited for the outraged husband outburst. But it did not come.

"I don't know." That simple statement somehow took the detective by surprise.

"Can I assume that if she had, Sergeant Rowley, that you would not have been very surprised?"

"Wouldn't be surprised at all, inspector."

"Why is that, sir?" Rowley shifted uncomfortably in his chair and was obviously deciding exactly what to say.

"As you probably know, Inspector Pollock, army wives should be seen and not heard. I can assure you mine wasn't like that. Helen had her favourite lost causes and she liked to sound off about them. She also had a very sweet voice and I liked to hear her, I must admit. I loved her and she loved me. Alright, I had to speak to her about it but only in a half-hearted sort of way for I knew she would ignore me anyway. She refused to turn a blind eye to anything she thought was unfair – and that was almost everything," Rowley added smiling. "Her outspokenness put the tin lid on my army career and no mistake. We split up constantly over it but not with any lingering animosity. She was just so lovely and kind. How could you be angry with someone who felt so deeply about folk worse off than herself? The thing is, I was actually so proud of her. I was just in the wrong occupation. I can't believe that she's dead? Who'll speak out for folk now?" The misery in Rowley's voice was palpable. "I can't believe she was in Glasgow and didn't get in touch with me."

"Sergeant Rowley, your wife had been living in this city since at least last October. She was earning her living as a primary school teacher."

"A teacher? How could she do that? I know she was studying to be one when I first met her but she was living with me since we married till last summer. How on earth could she get a post like that? She had no real qualifications and was as honest as the day was long. Why would she lie about that? Surely she needed some certificates to get a job as a teacher?" The questions were coming thick and fast and Pollock raised his hand to stop the flow.

"Let's go back to the beginning, sergeant, and let me ask the questions. Did your wife know a Miss Andrea Colquhoun?" Rowley started visibly at the mention of Andrea Colquhoun's name. His fingers tore at the handkerchief in his hand.

"What has that got to do with Helen collapsing in the street?"

"Questions, Sergeant Rowley, I'm trying to be very logical about all this, to get the relationships of people who might be involved into their correct slots. Now, did your wife know her?"

"Yes." Short and to the point.

"Now you've asked me what that has to do with your wife's death. Possibly nothing at all but it was Miss Colquhoun's teaching certificates that your wife used to obtain the teaching post. That makes me wonder just how she managed to get them. Were they misappropriated or did Miss Colquhoun simply give them to her?"

"Better ask Andrea Colquhoun, not me," came the barbed reply. Pollock let silence reign for a few minutes.

"Were they close friends?"

"I don't know."

"Where and when did the first meet, can you tell me that?"

"In Hong Kong. I was stationed there."

"And what was Miss Colquhoun doing there?"

"She was there with her family. They're a circus act and were performing in Hong Kong."

"For the troops?"

"No."

"So how did you and your wife meet her?"

"At a sort of garden party, all very informal."

"And, Sergeant Rowley, did the invitation come to you or your wife?"

"To me. Just a large group of people who met up for a drink and a chat. Nothing, no reason in particular."

"And Miss Colquhoun was there?" Rowley nodded.

"She was performing with her family. Just a mini version of their act, more acrobatics than any part of their actual act. It was just a large party, one of many the people stationed out there give to stave off the boredom."

"Then, I presume, the circus moved on?"

"They did."

"But Miss Colquhoun didn't?" asked Pollock giving the impression he already knew the answer. Rowley squirmed slightly.

"Would you like some water, sir?" asked Quigley, thinking it now quite safe to look up. Rowley shook his head.

"I just can't take it in that Helen's dead."

"Did Miss Colquhoun move on?" asked Pollock once more.

"No, she managed to get permission to stay on for a few weeks from the authorities."

"Sergeant Rowley, exactly what was your own relationship with Miss Colquhoun then and now?" Pollock asked bluntly.

"We were lovers." Quigley blushed a very unbecoming puce.

"Were or are?"

"Both." Quigley let his thoughts stray into the oncoming struggle against Rangers FC in the Charity Cup Final.

"Then you'll know how we can contact her?"

"No. The word 'are' is not quite accurate. It had run its course but I know she won't take that for the truth."

"And you were going back to your wife?"

"No again. She wouldn't have me, and before you jump to conclusions, I was telling the truth when I said I didn't know she was in Glasgow. I wrote to her family home in Liverpool but the letter wasn't answered." Not surprised, thought Pollock sourly.

"Maybe she didn't get it. Anyway, can you tell me how Mrs Rowley got hold of these qualifications? Did you have any of Andrea Colquhoun's papers?"

"No, none."

"When did you last see Miss Colquhoun?"

"Last August. She was leaving for China to do some missionary work."

"That must have been a very short stay for she was last seen in Bosworth Street in Tollcross just over a week ago. Could you have another try at thinking about her personal papers, Sergeant Rowley?" The tension was beginning to rise in that little room, Pollock's face was expressionless and Austin Quigley had now completely forgotten who it was he hoped would play at centre-forward for Celtic on Saturday.

"Helen must have gotten them from me."

"Are you not certain?"

"Alright," spat out Rowley, "that's the only way possible. Andrea knew that I was being seconded to another regiment for two years. It had just gone to Hong Kong. She decided that the cheapest way to get there was to volunteer for the mission station in Macao but jump ship when it docked in Hong Kong. We would meet up and she would take Helen's place in the married quarters. She didn't need her teaching qualifications any more so she left them with me to get rid of. Helen must have discovered them and just took them."

"Did Mrs Rowley know about the two of you?"

"Probably. I don't know why she thought it was serious. She knew I wouldn't have gone through with it."

"So what happened to the Hong Kong plans?"

"The secondment was cancelled. Andrea had already sailed but you've just told me she's back." Quigley decided that Saturday's team selection was a much simpler affair and much more interesting. "She'll be mad as hell, probably."

"So I take it you have not been in touch since she returned?" asked Pollock.

"No, it's over. I'm not interested." Neither was Pollock now but he reminded himself that he was being paid to be.

"Does she know you're in the barracks?"

"There's no way she can." You hope, thought both detectives.

"The group you associated with outwith your regiment, I'd like to mention a few names to see if you recognise any of them as being part of it. Miles McMaster." Pollock let the name sink in.

"Yes, I know McMaster. He worked for Jardine Matheson. There was a pile of money to be made working for them."

"And McMaster also knew Miss Colquhoun?"

"Yes."

"What was your relationship with him?" Rowley shrugged.

"Nothing in particular. I heard he'd trained as an architect but had run into some kind of bother back home. That's all."

"Did his cousin, Peter Yair, get him a job with Jardine Matheson?"

"I think so. He could speak Cantonese so he was retained as an interpreter. So I heard anyway."

"And Peter Yair, did you know him well?"

"You obviously know I did."

"How close were you to him?"

"He was a casual sort of friend like McMaster. The regiment is a soldier's life as well you know."
"And how about opium?" Pollock suddenly threw that into the mix.
"What?" Rowley's face was ashen.
"Opium." Pollock said the word as if it were chocolate.
"Nothing like that ever surfaced where I was, absolutely nothing. You mention that outside that door and I'll be out on my ear before the day's out. I've never had anything to do with that and I never saw any of it on the go at any garden party or meeting I was at. The slightest hint of that could see my life shot to pieces. For God's sake, watch what you're saying." Rowley looked as if his life was teetering on a knife-edge. Pollock changed tack while Rowley was still in shock.
"Peter Yair. Where were you when he was brutally assaulted? He died from those injuries, in case you didn't know. This is a murder enquiry and your deceased wife was a resident in his boarding-house."
"When did it happen?"
"On Wednesday of this week, in the evening." Rowley was greatly relieved at that news.
"Count me out for I was on Dartmoor until noon yesterday. I only got back here two hours ago. I can prove that, obviously. The army has all the necessary paperwork."
"One final question, Sergeant Rowley, have you ever been in touch with Peter Yair, Andrea Colquhoun or Miles McMaster recently?"
"Definitely not. The last person among them that I spoke to was Andrea and that was last summer." Rowley looked and sounded as if he had been put through the mill. Pollock stood up and Quigley followed his lead, closing his notebook as silently as he could.
"Thank you for your co-operation, Sergeant Rowley. If I were you, I'd stick to regimental life. At least there you know who your ememies are and your friends really are just

that." With that, Pollock and Quigley left Maryhill Barracks and met Jacobstein just outside the gates.

Jacobstein's expression said it all.

"What now, Jake?" asked his boss, his heart sinking.

"Miles McMaster has hanged himself from the transept of a Celtic cross in the Necropolis."

Chapter 7

The Necroplis was swarming with policemen. Inspector McLachlan was supervising but came over as soon as he saw Pollock enter the City of the Dead.

“All a bit over the top, is it not?” said Pollock. “Suicide is usually a quiet affair to save the relatives more distress than is necessary. “It certainly is, Ben, but this death is now a murder enquiry.”

“What?” asked Pollock speechless, Jacobstein was not.

“Dr McPherson? What makes him think so?” The sergeant was gazing round but there was no sight of the medical man.

“Bruising. Finger marks on the neck. He thinks Miles McMaster was rendered unconscious by someone exerting pressure on his neck and then strung up.”

“That someone would have to be helluva strong to manage that.”

“My point exactly, but Dr McPherson says it’s not impossible if McMaster was standing on the raised platform surrounding the cross he was hanging from. All it needed, says he, with McMaster having lean frame, was to hold him upright, put the noose around his neck and then over the transept and let him go. His sagging weight would do the rest.”

“With the killer holding on like hell till he could tie the rope to the granite,” finished Pollock. “Nonsense!”

“Exactly,” said McLachlan. “The body’s been taken to the morgue on the order of your superintendent. He said you were in the Maryhill Barracks. Think he’s hoping you were joining up,” said McLachlan subduing, with difficulty, a smile.

“Can’t say it didn’t cross my mind.”

“Well, he says it’s in your hands, says it’s probably all to do with the case you’re already working on.”

“That dead man was hale and hearty when Jake and I left him just over an hour ago and he was looking forward to spending the packet he'd just inherited from our previous murder victim."

"Good God! It's maybe just as well my family, including myself, are all just about skint."

"I'll have a look round the scene of the crime, then I'll head back to the office in Camlachie."

"Glad you've arrived, Ben. If we can do anything to help, just let me know."

"Will do."

For a while, Pollock just lurked about the 12' tall Celtic cross and let his mind take in nothing but the atmosphere. On a dark night, it would certainly be frightening, but the atmosphere that day, despite the slight drizzle now falling, was one that implied that the dead were actually having quite a happy time. That was probably because the air was full of stone angels with flapping wings, happy angels with mesmerising smiles and light-footed nympths, well-built and barely clothed, standing on tip-toe and appearing ready to pounce on the first person who gave them a backward glance. It quite took a body's mind off death. There was too much activity, not enough sombreness. Pollock made much of his salary through sudden deaths, so he was definitely on the side of doom and gloom graveyards.

"Austin, get a report from every one of these men who've been searching or asking around. Tell them the reports have to be written and detailed. Actual facts are to be listed as such and impressions under that heading. Jake, see that table grave, the one that looks like a bench? Well it was, in a way, made for you and me. Let's stake a claim to it and discuss this most unfortunate development." They made for a raised, flat tombstone and sat down to think. The drizzle had more or less gone but it was still solemnly overcast, any brighter clouds being quickly absorbed by heavy, grey, black ones. Pollock realised, too late, that the stone was wet, Jacobstein did not. He managed to suppress a laugh.

"Right," said Pollock, "that's it, Camlachie. A cab and I'll pay."

The small office was warm, the even smaller fire was still active enough to dry Pollock's trousers. Although it was the end of May, it was unseasonably cold and wet. Pollock finally sat down and the heat from his clothing as it met the material of the chair, suddenly zoomed through his entire body and life was sweet again. The tea and Carla's pastries added a sublime sense of unreality.

"Right, boys, still on a murder investigation but they've given us another body just to stave off the boredom as Sergeant Rowley would say. This time it's Miles McMaster who has managed to become dead and rich at the same time. He was rich because he inherited outright all of Peter Yair's estate of all description and dead because somebody was either simply jealous or wanted rid of him permanently. All we have to discover is who that person is."

"Along with whoever helped Yair to depart this life," added Jacobstein scooping the crumbs of his pastry into his hands and tossing them into the bin at the side of the desk.

"That's correct, Jake. It's all quite simple. One and one make two. Well, bearing in mind the fact that we know nothing at all about who actually did Yair in, it seems we might just as well be saying the same about McMaster this time tomorrow."

"I'll be at the game, sir," said Quigley and promptly wished he had kept his mouth shut as his boss slowly shook his head.

"No you won't," said Pollock solemnly, and that, Quigley knew, was the death knell sounding the end of his hopes of seeing Celtic win the three cups. "Now let's see what we know about McMaster yet again. You first, Jake, and I'll take notes."

"He was a cousin of the deceased Peter Yair. He was also a failed architect who got a job as an interpreter through his aforementioned cousin. We don't know why they both packed in their jobs or if, in fact, they were sacked by

Jardine Matheson in Hong Kong. We could follow that up, Ben."

"Excellent idea."

"McMaster was extremely upset when he learned his cousin had died. Quite a natural reaction, though, for they seemed to be on good terms. He was married to Gina Brossi and was helping out at the café on the High Street. He also knew Nigel Rowley, Helen Rowley and Andrea Colquhoun but they were not close now although, they, with Peter Yair, were friends in Hong Kong. He seemed fine in the café when we interviewed him but shortly after, he was found hanging from a Celtic cross in the Necropolis just off the High Street. Murder."

"Thanks, Jake. Now, to me he seemed no more that a dim lad but my impression is that somebody was aware that McMaster knew something that could hang that person. Now who could that person be and what could McMaster have known? Give me the answer to those questions, Austin, and you can get out your green and white scarf." Quigley looked desolate, Jacobstein continued relentlessly.

"The only two of the Hong Kong group remaining are Nigel Rowley and Andrea Colquhoun. Now it could also be someone with absolutely no connection with that group. McMaster said that Yair the Pimp was involved in many things or rackets as we might term them, but we've no idea what. What I'd like to know is why somebody would leave all his money and property to a man who thought him a despicable bastard?"

"Quite correct. Let's take McMaster first as that killer's trail is still hot or would be if we could only find out where McMaster went after he left us, Jake. Had he intended going out? Was it something we said that startled him? Did his wife know of a previous engagement? That question will be the beginning of this enquiry. If he did have an appointment, who was it with?"

"That person must have come with a rope and had predetermined to kill our victim. Consequently, I don't think the killer would have written a letter making the appointment and signed it. Anyway, who on earth makes an appointment to meet in a graveyard? Also, if things between the two of them were very confidential, I don't see our Miles confiding in Gina,"said Jacobstein.

"Well, we might just as well ask her anyway. It's another cab-ride for you Austin, and as we – or at least some of us – are on the count-down to Celtic's first treble-trophy season, no messing about. Bring Gina and Carla here and then when we're finished, take them back to that café. It's Enzo's. I think Jake and I will have a word with Miss Columbine after that."

"I know the name of the café, sir, for it's marked on the paper bag."

"Shades of JAE, Austin. Publicity's everything." Jacobstein laughed as Pollock spoke. Austin Quigley had a lot riding on an early conclusion to this case so he moved fast out of the office.

Both Pollock and Jacobstein spent the next five minutes writing.

"What I'm left with after a good five minutes' intensive thinking is this, Jake. We have a group of five, three of them now deceased. We haven't even seen never mind interviewed Andrea Colquhoun and that's what we should do as soon as we can find out where she is. Her folks won't tell us where Andrea Colquhoun is, so what do we do?"

"Well, Ben, as we're going back to Bosworth Street, I reckon you'll be asking Miss Columbine to think very deeply. Stroll down memory lane, perhaps."

"That girl Colquhoun is around here somewhere. She's a trapeze artist as well as an acrobat. These circus people are exceptionally fit and fearless. They have to be if they're up on that very high trapeze and one mistake is almost certainly fatal or at best, life-changing," said Pollock, his admiration clearly showing in his tone of voice. “They say it’s all about timing, confidence in your partner and your partner’s strong arms. I think we really do need to bring Miss Colquhoun in here for a lengthy chat.”

“But why would she do it, Ben?”

“I’ve no idea. Maybe she and McMaster were running some scam together. Actually, I haven’t really got a clue but we do need to rule her out at the very least.” A knock at the door and Sergeant Hanley appeared note in hand.

“Two in one, Ben. Dr McPherson popped in to say that Helen Rowley’s death is now officially classified as due to natural causes and that Dr Jeffrey has decided that he’d have more success finding gold in a fish supper than absolute proof of his still-held opinion. He’s contemplating emigrating to Australia.” The door closed again and all was silent.

“Thank God for that in both cases. Plenty of gold in Australia, too, I’m told.”

“He’s actually quite brilliant, Ben, as a scientist. Pity if he does go,” said Jacobstein and meant it.

“He’s talking his usual load of tripe. He’s almost emigrated to every country in the known world and to one or two he just suspects exist. We’ll take him out to drown his sorrows when we find the swine who killed both Yair and his cousin.” Pollock shook his head and stood up as Jacobstein spoke again.

“You don’t think Gina Brossi killed her husband, do you, Ben? She’s his next-of-kin and unless he’s left a will saying otherwise, she gets the lot.”

“Right first time. Now I’m off to the lavatory and then a quick chat to Hanley to see if any of his men imparted any little gems to him that were not in their reports. Gossip is my lifeline at the moment. Everything else is going nowhere. I’ll remain downstairs and bring the female members of the Brossi clan up here when they arrive. You get on with writing up your notes, Jake." With that, DI Pollock left.

Jacobstein was just re-reading the final draft of his report when he heard voices on the stairs. He had already arranged the chairs in what he termed Ben Pollock order. The Italian ladies swept into the room.

"Enzo's watching the shop," Carla announced to Jacobstein. His clothes apparently demanded respect.

"In safe hands, I'm sure," he mumbled. Carla didn't look so sure. It was quite obvious who actually ran the business. Jacobstein gently guided the new widow to the most comfortable seat in the office, but that wasn't saying much. Pollock took his own seat whilst Jacobstein and Quigley settled down in the background.

"Words can't explain how sorry we are at what has happened to your husband, Mrs McMaster. We are doing everything we can to bring his murderer to justice." Especially as it's getting mighty close to kick-off, thought Quigley anxiously. Carla shared his sentiments in a manner of speaking.

"Would you mind just getting to the point, Inspector Pollock, for I've a business to run and the death of one dishonest, lazy swine seems to me to come a poor second to making money to keep my family alive."

"Well, Mrs Rossi, one of your family has just died and."

"Not my family and not my Gina's," said the lady, shaking her head decisively. "That profligate git was more bother than he was worth and Gina knows it." Gina stopped snivelling and agreed.

"A waster. I thought I was stuck with him for life." Jacobstein, a romantic at heart, looked up quickly from his note-taking and only just managed to delete his look of disapproval in time. Pollock had known what his colleague's reaction would be and managed to divert the ladies' attention at the last minute. Jacobstein, he thought, was one of the few men left in the city over the age of twenty-five who thought marriage would be a bowl of cherries. He groaned inwardly at Gina's statement and sincerely hoped he did not have another two murder suspects.

"Could you tell us, Mrs McMaster, a little about your husband's private life, please? What kind of man he was, for example, his interests, that sort of thing?" Carla Brossi looked like she could do a first-rate job of character assassination and he hoped Gina would not hold back out of some kind of wifely loyalty.

"I thought I had already summed him up, Inspector Pollock. A waster, a ne'er-do-well, a scrounger, hopeless in every area, and a womaniser which I must confess gives me a laugh. Yes, gentlemen, that one surprised me , too. Just goes to show that there are women in Glasgow who have no taste."

"Not universally popular then, Mrs McMaster? said Pollock thoughtfully, thoroughly enjoying the lady's refreshing take on marriage.

"Call me Miss Gina Brossi. To be perfectly frank, that toad was very popular with women who were either way too old, too desperate or too lazy to be bothered looking around." Pollock wondered why she had married McMaster, for Gina Brossi was a dark-eyed beauty, lustrous black hair falling in thick, undulating waves over her shoulders, nobody's fool and she answered his unspoken question without hesitation. She smiled broadly. "I was offered a partnership in a chip-shop, McMaster had money then and I needed it. Turns out he was a man with a big mouth and a small wallet."

"A lazy sponger," put in Carla just in case her daughter had deliberately missed that one out. Gina sneezed quite delicately into her lace handkerchief. Jacobstein was impressed.

"Sorry about that," she said putting the white lace away, "got a slight cold." That accounted for the snivelling, thought Pollock. "Hobbies, none, didn't have any. And that, gentlemen, is the most honest obituary you'll hear."

"Miss Brossi," said Pollock who learned fast, "your husband left the café after speaking to us. As he was doing some stock-taking for your father, did he leave on café business?" Gina shook her head and looked as if she thought Pollock was mad.

"My father wouldn't have trusted him to fill a cone with ice-cream far less do any work for him when he wasn't right under his eyes. But I'll tell you why he left." Jacobstein, Quigley and Pollock listened intently. "He received a note just as we were opening the café this morning and from the look on his all too vacant face, it was a most satisfactory communication. It was also from a woman."

"Did you see the note, what was written there?"

"No, I don't read intimate communications and I assumed it was that. Besides, men don't or, I should say, didn't take to him. He took the note with him but I saw enough to know it was a woman's handwriting. It was obviously an assignation. When, where or why I don't know but an educated guess says it was in the Necropolis. As good a place to meet your maker as any, I suppose. Poetic justice, maybe."

"I don't suppose you know the name of his latest conquest?" asked Pollock and he hoped he had not been too brutal.

"No idea, I'm afraid, but at a guess I'd say it was just another of his sleazy, unsuccessful business deals as he didn't steal a box of chocolates. We're now short of a bottle of chianti."

"Do you know anything about a group of friends he made while he worked in Hong Kong some time ago? Did you ever meet any of them?" Carla was beginning to get restless and Gina took the hint.

"Not much and I never met any of them."

"Not even his cousin, Peter Yair?"

"McMaster said Yair was an unsavoury customer – the pot calling the kettle black – and not the kind of person a man would introduce to his wife."

"He didn't elaborate as to what Mr Yair's unsavoury activities were?"

"I'm afraid not."

"Your husband assumed that he was the late Peter Yair's heir."

"Did he? Was he? Now that might have been a colossal windfall for me inasmuch as I might have seen the back of him for good. Occasionally, I've thought of paying him to stay away. No need now. As they say, it's an ill wind that blows nobody good. If he was indeed worth money and I get it, it'll go entirely to the poor for that selfish apology for a man gave them nothing while he lived. I'd sooner starve than take one penny that was his. Mama says you liked my cakes, gentlemen, so to celebrate my getting out of jail so to speak, I'll send you a complimentary selection of them tomorrow."

"Excuse me, Miss Brossi, could you make that today?" said Quigley, "for you see, I'm going to the Charity Cup Final tomorrow and there will be none left by the time I get back."

Gina shook her head sadly.

"Sorry, but I like my gifts to be fresh-made. But, I'll send a few over later this afternoon especially for you." Pollock gave in.

"That's very kind of you, Miss Brossi. We'll certainly enjoy them for we eat very irregularly while we're on a case. Just one last thing. About that Hong Kong group. Did you ever hear the names Nigel and Helen Rowley or Andrea Colquhoun mentioned?" Gina thought for a moment while Carla picked up her bag.

"Rowley, no, I've never heard that name. The Colquhoun one, yes. There was some connection with a circus. He mentioned it when a circus was here for the Christmas season. Nothing else."

"That's all then, ladies. You've been very helpful. DC Quigley will take you back to the High Street in a cab." And no doubt pick up his pastries while he was at it, Pollock thought hopefully. He saw them downstairs and into the cab. Jacobstein looked a little shocked when Pollock returned to the office.

“The lady’s now available, Jake, but I think she’s a little too independent for you to cope with.”

“I think I might just take a chance on that, Ben. Life would certainly not be boring.” His boss thought that was the understatement of the year.

Pollock and Jacobstein alighted from the tram and walked the few hundred yards to Boworth Street before turning down it and heading for Peter Yair’s boarding-house. The garden had been tidied up to within an inch of its life and the windows were gleaming. It looked like McMaster had either splashed out in anticipation of his inheritance being confirmed or had been told to erase the remains of the trashing before the ‘For Sale’ sign could be put up when he officially owned the property.

“Do you think Miss Columbine will have given this matter any kind of serious thought, Ben?”

“Almost certainly. The circus and the music hall are all part of the performing arts and Miss Columbine understands that when she talks to us, she’s on show. She’ll have been wracking her brain, and Mr Pierot’s too, I should think, for any little bit that could serve as an encore for her last performance.” Their luck was in. Miss Columbine was in the boarding-house’s sitting-room. Most of the other occupants, including the cook, seemed to be out. She sat in her favourite armchair and looked like the Queen of the May, the detectives being her courtiers. She was dressed to kill and she looked every inch a stage performer. Her long earrings sparkled, her rings flashed and she herself glittered with delight. Both Pollock and Jacobstein smiled back.

“And what may I do for you two boys today? Have you heard that Mr Yair’s heir is going to sell? But I just don’t see it happening as I told Cecil Snowball. I’m sure that Mr

McMaster will see that this house has an excellent reputation and realise that it means a steady, reliable income."

"I'm afraid he won't, Miss Columbine," said Pollock quietly.

"But surely when."

"I'm afraid the gentleman is dead." Miss Columbine slowly slumped in her chair, speechless. But suddenly she found her voice.

"Mr Snowball!" she screetched, "oh Mr Snowball, he's dead! He's dead!" Jacobstein rose and opened the sitting-room door and moved on into the hallway.

"Mr Snowball, sir, are you there? This is Detective Sergeant Jacobstein. Miss Columbine has had some bad news and she's asking for you. Would you come down to the sitting-room as soon as possible? Detective Inspector Pollock is also here." He waited until he heard an upstairs door opening and then returned to where Miss Columbine was sipping some sherry, poured from a bottle with her name on it.

"Would you pour Mr Snowball a little brandy from his own bottle, please, Inspector Pollock? He'll be shocked, too. The glasses are on the small table beside it."

Cecil Snowball entered the room, his face etched with concern for his fellow resident. He took the seat next to Miss Columbine and gently patted her hand.

"What on earth are you saying, Collie, who's dead? Not your own Mr Pierot, surely. He's a healthy type of man, looks after himself when he's not in the pub." Miss Columbine shook her head very slowly and then burst into tears.

"Oh not my Mr Pierot, Cecil, it's Mr McMaster. He's dead they say. What shall we all do? Where shall we all go?"

"God save us! Is he?" Mr Snowball asked. "A brainstorm, was it? Always thought he was a bit highly-strung, always getting het up about nothing, wasn't he, Collie? But a nice lad, just the same. Terrible news for his family, I expect." Mr Snowball took a large gulp of his brandy.

"Italians they are, his in-laws," said Miss Columbine. "I once worked with an Italian equestrian act. Well, not exactly worked with them, not actually part of their act. We were all members of the same circus. Roeburton's American Circus. Very dramatic the Italians were, very clever, very flamboyant. Oh, Mr Snowball, looks like our futures are uncertain yet again."

"Never mind, Collie. I might buy it and I've got a wife who can come in here and run the place. She'd like that. The kids are getting on a bit and can stay with their granny. All's well that ends well." Pollock knew that facts had to be faced.

"I'm afraid it wasn't natural causes, Cecil. We've had three sudden deaths all linked to here in a way. You'll both be glad to know that Miss Rowley's was perfectly natural. Heart failure." A heavy silence followed this announcement. Cecil Snowball shook his head sadly.

"Far too young to be taken." Mr Snowball sipped his brandy thoughtfully.

"Too soon," said Miss Columbine deep in her own sad thoughts. Pollock let the unhappy silence reign for a moment or two before speaking once more.

"The reason we're here really is to find out a bit more, if we can, of the whereabouts of Miss Andrea Colquhoun. We wondered if you might help us, Miss Columbine. There's no need for you to leave, Mr Snowball." Mr Snowball took a long look at Miss Columbine's distressed features and decided to stay.

"What would you like to know in particular, Mr Pollock?"

"I was wondering if you've been in touch with her or her family in the recent past?"

"I've been thinking about that," the lady said softly, putting her sherry glass onto a little side-table. "It's been on my mind a great deal. Andrea's been here a few times to see Peter Yair and her parents have come to see me perform in the theatre. Now that was about seven weeks ago in Wishaw.

We've known each other for decades and circus people never forget each other, We're very faithful. In the circus, we all work very hard. As you can imagine, it's a hard life with all that travelling, but the comradeship is first-class. I've been trying to think where you might find Andrea. Her mother's very close to her so you'll get nothing from her if Andrea has indicated she doesn't want to be found. I do know that Andrea met both Mr Yair and Mr McMaster when she was with the family out in Hong Kong. It might sound odd to you, but almost all British circuses are international. That is to say, they've been travelling to places such as Russia, Australia, the USA, Europe, you name it for all of this century and I've worked in all of them. I was actually born in Berlin."

"And has anything come to mind, Miss Columbine?" asked Pollock quietly.

"Yes, I'm happy to say. The last time I saw her, she left in a right temper. Oh, she wasn't coming here to see me. I heard her say to Mr Yair, 'All right, Number 9 Lavender Street. Be there.' Whether that is where she's living or not, I don't know." The detectives were lifted right out of their despondency and into seventh heaven. An address recently connected with Andrea Colquhoun and the street where Peter Yair had been assaulted. Pollock could have kissed the lovely Miss Columbine and Jacobstein wondered where Gina Brossi liked to eat on a night out.

Chapter 8

There was a heavy police presence outside the McMasters' flat in Alloa Place, the address listed in the Post Office directory as belonging to them, and quite a crowd had gathered to watch the frolics. They had actually got McMaster's address, though, from the Brossis. Gina had refused to come as she insisted she lived over the café and had never been inside the place. It seemed McMaster had moved between Alloa Place and Bosworth Street at will. One of the occupants had been murdered and that meant it was fair game for the gossips living nearby. The street was a short one consisting of three closes on either side, the whole affluent-looking and the blonde-stone buildings well maintained.

The flat was full of police and empty of occupants. Austin Quigley stood in the very middle directing traffic.

"Took a while to find his address, sir, as the Brossi family were already at the undertakers ordering a small but tasteful funeral so as to be ready for the off when they're given the thumbs up from the officials in charge. All done and dusted but on hold."

"Who's watching the shop?" asked Pollock.

"Two nephews who generally help run two of the other cafes, one in Bothwell Street and the other in Sauchiehall Street near Charing Cross Mansions. A very large family, it seems are the Brossis. All now bought and paid for even before the insurance policies are handed in. Don't think he was well-liked, sir," added Quigley.

"So the funeral notice definitely won't say 'sadly missed'?" commented Pollock.

"Goodbye and good riddance?" suggested Jacbstein.

"In Italian, of course, for it's the kind of language that sounds caressing if you don't actually know what it means.

"Should maybe be in Cantonese," said Jacobstein, "as that seems to be his only saleable point."

"That's a good thought for this is the age of expansion and we should celebrate the knowledge that Glasgow has produced a failed, Cantonese-speaking architect who, had he been any good at his first job, might never have had the chance to exercise the second. Now that reminds me, we have to find out why those two left Hong Kong. Resigned, sacked or what? Trot round to Jardine Matheson's, Austin. Their headquarters are here in the city and find out. They keep a stern eye on their employees for big money means big temptation to line pockets in an unofficial way. You know something, I wouldn't mind a job with them myself and it would only be a few thousand miles from my in-laws in New Delhi. That would set me up for life. Off you go, Austin, and don't let the marble staircases put you off. Those millionaires all put their drawers on one leg at a time like the rest of us."

Pollock and Jacobstein split up as the uniformed branch moved out to let them have a free-hand.

"Are we looking for anything in particular, Ben, or just anything at all that ties in with McMaster's death and his cousin Yair's?"

"That's about it, Jake. Anything to do with Yair, the others and dear old Hong Kong. There might be something of interest to do with our mysterious school-teacher cum acrobat, Miss Andrea Colquhoun. Ah, look at this. The ubiquitous locked desk. Keys out, Jake, and do your stuff, but I think this looks like an insult to your renowned expertise. This desk looks like the face of the man it belonged to – bland."

"Gina said vacant, if I remember correctly."

"She did and you do. When you make her your ever-loving wife, Jake, remind me to be a thousand miles away for I hate to see a man metaphorically chucking himself under a tram."

Jake Jacobstein only laughed for he had heard it all before.

"Now," he said, "from where I'm standing, I can see that this little desk is not a one minute job. In fact, Ben, we might have to call in an expert."

"Right now, Jake, all the experts are having their morning coffee in Barlinnie Jail, so, if all else fails, use that screwdriver he keeps in this odds and ends drawer I've just opened. In fact, just do that right now and don't be too fussy about the damage. This is a murder investigation and the owner is in no condition to complain. No time to lose." The resulting snap could be heard a mile off and the lid of the desk was released.

"Think that's solved the problem, Ben." Jacobstein replaced the screwdriver.

"What a shocking state of affairs. If McMaster's architectural drawings resembled this paper carnage, he should have been permanently excluded from his profession." The pigeon-holes were simply crammed with papers, letters just either crumbled or torn up to over-flowing. The paper supply simply flowed like a river in flood as it was released. Jacobstein picked up handfuls off the carpet and glanced quickly through them. He was a very neat man and this careless shambles offended him. Pollock found the side drawers of this knee-hole desk open and in much the same state.

"Is that Felix Tiffney's voice I hear on the stairs, Jake?" Jacobstein nodded but didn't stop searching for a moment through the mess of paper before him. He was quick and accurate. "Right then, we'll leave this to Felix. He'll be even faster than you for he intends going to the Cup Final tomorrow along with Austin. Felix!" Pollock yelled and Tiffney appeared almost at once.

"Here, Boss," said the bluff Irishman, "what would you like me to do?"

"That lot."

"Burn it?"

"No."

"Aw hell!"

"Well put. All you have to do is cast your eyes over every single piece of it, long or short, and look out for any reference to the names Sergeant Rowley, Helen Rowley, Andrea Colquhoun, Miles McMaster and Peter Yair. The name of Hong Kong will almost certainly crop up so put it all aside with the above names. If anything strikes you as particularly odd or incriminating bearing in mind that the last two have been murdered in the past few days, give me a shout. We'll be at Camlachie police office in an hour or two, so wait for us there when you're finished here. Keep your hands off any Italian pastries you might find in my office and make a full written report about what you find in amongst that lot and in any other place in this flat. The flat belongs to the late Miles McMaster."

"He was found dead in the Necropolis, wasn't he?" Pollock nodded and made for the door. "Right then, Ben," said Sergeant Tiffney, the latest to be seconded to the team on a temporary basis, "I'll get started and see you later. What pastries?"

"A personal gift from Mrs McMaster to Quigley but she really meant me and Jake as well. She's well-taken with our interviewing methods and regards our gentle way of breaking the sad news of her husband's death to her as being in the top tier of the caring police force. This is her way of celebrating, as she would put it, now being as free as a bird."

"Sounds like she's a fine woman, so she does. There's nothing like a woman who can face facts and see the best in them." DS Tiffney looked unduly solemn and thoughtful.

"Too late, Felix, keep your patter for somebody else. Jake's beaten you to it." Jacobstein ignored both of them.

"Ah well, a wee bit of pastry will go some way to consoling me and Austin's a very generous boy." With that, Tiffney took himself and his disappointment off to work on the mammoth paper task and Pollock and Jacobstein headed downstairs.

The crowd outside was silent as Pollock stopped beside a uniformed constable, one of two patrolling outside the tenement building.

"The door out of the back close has been locked now by the landlord, sir."

"Too many chancing their arms, constable?"

"Yes, sir. A lady was here while you were inside and she asked me to tell you that if you have a spare moment in your very busy life, would you care to call round and see her for a few moments?"

"Let me tell you, constable. Sorry, what's your name?"

"McCallum, sir, Angus McCallum," answered the young Highlander.

"Now, Constable McCallum, never turn down any plea, however insignificant it might seem, from a lady, especially one who can appreciate the fact that the police force in this city is chronically underpaid and undermanned. I presume she left her name and address?"

"She did, sir. She's the Reverend Alan Carson's wife and they live next door to the Jerusalem Mission church in Lavender Street. She's Mrs Adele Carson."

"Thank you, Constable McCallum, Now tell me if you can, is Lavender Street where Mrs Carson lives and Mr Peter Yair was assaulted close by?"

"Two quite long streets away, sir. When you get off the tram outside the public library, cross the street and it's the first on your left."

"My thanks, constable." Pollock walked over to where Jacobstein had stopped.

"Our next step would appear to be the mission church house in Lavender Street. Mrs Carson wants a word. Strange that street should figure several times in our enquiries. I wonder what the lady has to tell us, Jake?"

"Must surely be about the mysterious Miss Colquhoun – I hope," added Jacobstein.

They jumped onto the first tram going their way and both stood by the winding stairs lost in thought. The streets were thronged with people going about their daily business and Pollock wondered if Andrea Colquhoun was walking about in amongst them, her conscience clear or muddied by the dirty waters her Hong Kong friends were steeped in. He was roused from his reverie as Jacobstein swung himself down onto the pavement as the tram ground slowly to a halt.

The Reverend Alan Carson stood up from his gardening labours as the two detectives approached him.

"Still labouring in God's vineyard, Mr Carson?" asked Jacobstein whose interest in that hobby was well-known.

"The labourer is worthy of his hire, Mr Jacobstein, and my price is a cup of tea and a few slices of paradise cake."

"Home-made?" Pollock could see his sergeant's devotion to Italian pastries vanishing.

"Quite so, Mr Jacobstein. Are you any farther on with your enquiries, Mr Pollock?"

"A set-back occurred this morning, sir. A friend of Mr Yair's was murdered in the Necropolis, I'm afraid. Complicates matters even further." The Reverend Carson's smile faded.

"What on earth's going wrong with the world? I don't see that the ordinary people round here are any different from what they've always been. Caring folk and a lot of them have a very hard time financially. They often seek comfort in drink and drink often fuels fueds. Always has been like that, I'm afraid. I try to encourage my folk to get involved in trade unions for I don't see any other way out of poverty." Mr Carson shrugged. "Some listen and some don't. Fear is at the bottom of it all for nobody can afford to lose a job. No money, no food, no life. But tell me, Mr Pollock, the newly-deceased was a friend of Mr Yair's, you said. Is that why you're involved in both cases?"

"Yes, sir. Now we're off to see your wife. She asked if we could pop in. Is she at home?"

"At home and hopefully taking the paradise cake out of the oven. The door's open. Just shout out your arrival as you go in. There's a good half-hour's weeding to be done before I take a rest for a bit."

The CID men walked twenty yards down the road past the mission hall itself and eventually came to the grey-stone house. Its small garden was immaculate and Jacobstein eyed that with pleasure and made a mental note to come back in the summer to admire what seemed to him to be a most adventurous partnering of plants.

"We'll keep this chat with Mrs Carson strictly to the point and then it's back to Camlachie. We have to find that girl and I'd like to know a lot about Peter Yair's unsavoury activities. We'll call Sergeant Rowley to Camlachie as soon as we get back there. Now get your mind off the marigolds, mate, and onto the murders. We'll have Tiffney there, too. He'll be finished by then. He has a manic look in his eye that might make Rowley have second thoughts if he gets riled."

"I just can't figure out how one person could possibly get McMaster onto that cross." Jacobstein's expression clouded.

"For God's sake, Jake, don't say Celtic cross when Tiffney and Quigley are about or their minds will be back on that match tomorrow." Both laughed and Pollock called out to let Mrs Carson know they had arrived.

The lady appeared at the kitchen door and the smell of baking drifted along to them in a most welcoming way.

"Hello, Mrs Carson, sorry if this is just a brief meeting but we're snowed under with the results of folk simply misbehaving," said Pollock apologetically.

"I know, but come on in and have some tea and cake. Miss Colquhoun has very kindly just popped in. I've persuaded her to talk to you and she's waiting in there. Andrea will pour the tea and I'll leave you all to it."

Pollock and Jacobstein stood stock-still for a very brief moment. Pollock finally found his voice.

"Come on, Jake." They entered a large kitchen. A family-sized oak table stood in the middle, six chairs ranged around it and a young woman of about twenty-five stood pouring tea. Her auburn hair was piled loosely about her pale face, her eyes the colour of tiger stone and they seemed to change as she glanced from one man to the other.

"Milk?" They both nodded. "Help yourselves to sugar." She cut some slices of what they recognised as paradise cake and put a slice for each of them on small violet tea-plates which matched the cups and saucers. The three of them sat down in silence until Pollock remembered the warrant cards.

"Good to see you, Miss Colquhoun," he began, "we had hoped to speak to you sooner but you've been proving difficult to track down." His voice had a hint of a hard edge to it.

"So Mrs Carson was telling me. But, here we are together now, so feel free to ask me anything that you think might help further your investigations into the deaths of two of my friends, Helen Rowley and Peter Yair."

"I'm afraid you've now lost three of them, Miss Colquhoun, as Miles McMaster, whom I believe was also a friend of yours in Hong Kong, died violently this morning." Andrea Colquhoun looked surprised but not unduly sad. Pollock had absolutely no idea if she actually was surprised or sad. There was something dead in those tiger eyes but perhaps that was simply how she was. She seemed to be a young woman who could certainly look after herself and he had the feeling that she had not been persuaded by Mrs Carson to wait to speak to him. This meeting, he was certain, had been arranged by Andrea Colquhoun on her own terms and her own choice of venue. What was the impression she wanted to convey or what information did she want to have from him? He made a subtle gesture to Jacobstein to keep absolutely quiet as she poured milk into her tea. He was going to have to handle this very sensitively if he was to come out of this on the winnng side.

"Mrs Carson is a wonderful baker, it seems. You won't mind if we eat while we talk, will you, Miss Colquhoun?" he asked.
"Certainly not, inspector. We can't insult the baker by leaving the cake forgotten on the plate." Jacobstein was already eyeing a second slice and was also missing his notebook which had been signalled in Pollock's look to be kept out of sight.
"Miss Colquhoun, am I right in thinking that you're a school-teacher?"
"Yes, I am."
"But you're not working as one at the moment, are you?"
"Not at the moment, no."
"Are you actually working, are you employed in any capacity at all?"
"No, not really. I have a four week stint starting a week on Monday. Being unemployed is not something I aspire to, Inspector Pollock. I was brought up to work hard, very hard, I might add. It was much harder learning my trade than learning how to be a teacher, I can assure you of that."
"And your occupation in ten or so days from now will be what, Miss Colquhoun?"
"As an acrobat. I've been spending the past few weeks finessing my skills."
"Not with your family?" Miss Colquhoun shook her head.
"No, with another act who've lost one of their numbers due to illness. Why did you assume it was not with my family?"
"Your mother told us that she had no idea where you were when we asked her a few days ago." Miss Colquhoun did not show any surprise. "I presume you're wondering why we were speaking to your mother?" Miss Colquhoun shrugged elegantly.
"It did cross my mind as being rather odd."
"Actually, considering the circimstances, it wasn't. We had been hoping that a member of your family would contact us, so we were glad when Mrs Colquhoun called in at

Camlachie police office, where we are temporarily based, wanting to speak to us."

"And Mother provided you with the required answers, did she, Inspector Pollock?" Andrea Colquhoun smiled knowingly.

"Not really," Pollock replied wondering just how many people this girl had already roped into her scheme. "But you are here now and answering quite frankly our questions. So, all's well that ends well, and it's very seldom mothers do co-operate when their children are involved."

"Forgive me for sounding somewhat puzzled, Mr Pollock, but I don't see how I am involved, or possibly could be involved, in a police enquiry."

"Involved inasmuch as once belonging to a group of friends while you were all living for a time, albeit in your case just for a few months, in Hong Kong." Andrea Colquhoun reached out for the sugar bowl and for the first time, Pollock noticed how strong her hands, and probably her forearms, were. The trapeze artist's legacy? She suddenly looked up.

"Oh yes, of course, Miles and Peter. I can't believe they're gone." She still had not asked what had happened to Miles McMaster. "What actually happened to Miles?" she asked suddenly as if having read Pollock's thoughts.

"He was found hanging from the transept of a monumental cross in the Necropolis." The tiger eyes remained asleep.

"Suicide! Doesn't surprise me for he was always highly-strung. I suppose that's was an unfortunate way to put it, Inspector Pollock." Pollock ignored that last remark.

"And you were living in his flat in Alloa Place."

"No, I wasn't. It was merely an accommodation address for me. I've been living with friends, different houses. I was a bit unsettled, didn't quite know what I wanted to do with my life."

"And this was how you felt after you returned from Hong Kong?" Pollock asked.

"Yes, that's right," agreed the woman quickly.

"Why did you return? Weren't you supposed to be going on to China to take up a post there as a missionary?"

"A teaching one mainly, yes."

"So why are you here and not there?" Both detectives were interested in that answer.

"Does that question have any relevance to your murder investigations, Inspector Pollock."

"Can't think of any other reason I might have for asking it, Miss Colquhoun. It's probably up to you to let me have a true answer and then I'll be able to judge." He waited while Andrea Colquhoun debated whether or not to bother answering. She did not look the slightest bit put out.

"When the ship docked in Hong Kong before proceding to Macao, there was a letter waiting for me. The ship had suffered engine trouble and we were a week late in arriving. The letter was from a circus colleague telling me about a fatal accident to a much-loved family member, so I simply took the first ship leaving Hong Kong for home. It was a stupid hoax and I don't know who was responsible but I'll leave no stone unturned until I do." And both detectives did not doubt that – well, they would have thought that if a little red light signalling danger had not lit up in each other's mind's eye.

"Miss Colquhoun," said Pollock, "did you know that your teaching certificates were being used by one of your Hong Kong friends?"

"I do now. Helen Rowley, wasn't it?"

"That's right. Have you any idea how she got hold of them?"

"None."

"Not even that she might have got them from her husband, your lover?" Andrea Colquhoun hesitated for a very brief moment before replying.

"Well, now that you mention it, yes, she could have taken them from him out of spite. When I decided to do missionary work, I cleared everything out that I thought I wouldn't need and I asked him to get rid of them for me.

Didn't work out that way but there's still time to take up my post in China. I'm not at all interested in what Rowley does. That affair has come and gone, inspector. No hard feelings on either side."

"So I gathered from Sergeant Rowley, Miss Colquhoun."

"You've interviewed him?" Pollock merely nodded. "He's a very honest man. I can't imagine he'd let his wife impersonate me."

"He knew nothing about it." Miss Colquhoun just shrugged, a little less elegantly this time.

"Still, you'll be able to retrieve your certificates from him eventually."

"No, I don't think I'll bother. I've moved on from being incarcerated in a school. It's difficult to get the circus life out of your blood when you've been born into it. Is that all now, Inspector Pollock?"

"Just one or two more questions. Have you met Sergeant Rowley since your return to the city?"

"I haven't and he's no longer in the army, I've been told. I don't know where he might be. Think it was Peter who told me. They were in touch, I believe."

"I can assure you that Mr Yair's information was wrong. What about any of the other Hong Kong group members then? Have you met any of them since you came back? How about the very accommodating Miles McMaster? You obviously kept in touch with him, Miss Colquhoun."

"Miles was a lovely man married to that harridan Gina Brossi!" Pollock was glad she was looking straight at him and not at Jacobstein. "Yes, we did keep in touch periodically."

"By post?"

"No."

"You met up?"

"Miles liked to watch me performing. He loved the freedom of the circus life. He didn't believe that it all didn't just happen but that a lot of years of continuous work went into it.

He was quite a simple man in many ways. He was completely dominated by that horrible man, Peter Yair. He just fell in with whatever scum like him suggested. Yair sailed very close to the wind on many occasions."

"Were there ever any suggestions that Peter Yair dabbled in prostitution, a high-class pimp, in other words?" Pollock saw a look of fury come and go at speed in her eyes.

"How do you know about that?"

"How do you know about that, Miss Colquhoun, would be more to the point? We can't reveal our sources. You obviously knew about it yet you still remained friends."

"He made a lot of money and the girls didn't starve. Anyway, as it generally happened at sporting gatherings outside of Glasgow, it was a case of out of sight, out of mind for me. Beside, it was only rumours. It had nothing to do with me."

"And yet you were going to be a missionary? What exactly were you bringing to a culture thousands of years older than the one you would be peddling out there?" asked Pollock, knowing he was veering off the subject.

"I did try to reason with him a few times in Hong Kong but it didn't do any good."

"Thought it was only rumours – rumours you chose to ignore?"

"There was a huge demand for it out there among the ex-pats. Money was a great temptation for him and there was plenty of that floating about among them ready to be snapped up. No sewer was too rank for Peter. He was loathsome. Miles finally persuaded him to come home and his aunt had also made a few financial promises. He finally succumbed when the Jardine Matheson management heard of his extra-mural activities and got the first boat home just ahead of a police warrant."

"I'm also informed that you went to see Mr Yair at the beginning of last week."

"That's right," the lady smirked, "asked to afternoon tea."

"And had a big row with him." Miss Colquhoun swallowed hard.

"Oh, that was nothing. He made one of his crude suggestions and I stormed out."

"Giving him your accommodation address?"

"Miles had said that if the pair of us had a go at talking some sense into him, it might work. I wasn't susceptible to his charms, Miles was. Yair didn't come."

"Where were you on the evening he died, Miss Colquhoun?"

"Which evening was that?"

"Wednesday of this week although he was actually found the following day."

"At the music-hall watching Miss Columbine and her dogs."

"Which one?"

"The Britannia."

"A great way to relax." Pollock smiled.

"She was a great inspiration in her circus days, Inspector Pollock." Pollock and Jacobstein stood up.

"Thank you, Miss Colquhoun. Where might we find you if we need to speak to you again?"

"In Bosworth Street. I've taken Helen Rowley's old room."

Chapter 9

Pollock sat with his elbows on the desk in his office and sighed deeply.

"Don't know how we'd survive without rolls and sausages and eggs or anything, in fact," he complained. "Would be good to sit down occasionally with a full plate of something and a knife and fork. So no joy as far as Jardine Matheson are concerned. Resigned and that's that. We'll get nothing else from them. Right, let's clear it all away and hear what Felix has to say."

"He hasn't arrived back yet, sir," said Austin Quigley, being yet again the bearer of bad news.

"Hasn't he? I thought the absence of any of Miss Gina Brossi's delicious pastries meant he had."

"Under lock and key, sir." Quigley was nobody's fool, thought Jacobstein.

"Really? And who's got the key?"

"Sergeant Hanley, sir."

"And the price?"

"One of the pastries. Miss Brossi gave me six."

"Then we still have something to look forward to. Has Sergeant Rowley arrived yet?" asked Pollock more in hope than expectation. He was well-acquainted with army rules and regulations.

"Nope. Army duties outwith the barracks, it seems. He'll be here when he can be released."

"Maryhill's restless natives being subdued, are they?" asked Pollock sourly.

"Think that's Tiffney now, Ben," said Jacobstein quietly. The door was thrown open and DS Felix Tiffney fell into the room.

"I'll see somebody's sacked if that rip in the linoleum's not fixed within the year," threatened Tiffney, still clutching a jute bag stuffed with notepaper. "You're my witnesses, boys."

"We are, so have a seat and tell us how you enjoyed reading other folk's letters."

"First of all, let me say that there was no sign of a woman living in that flat. That is not to say there was no sign of a female presence, but just that it only came in the form of letters. Any tea going?" Quigley answered the call. "No matter what Gina Brossi says, there must have been something about him that roped the ladies in." Tiffney pulled a large bundle tied tightly with string out of the bag and there were plenty more still in it. He held the bundle up with both hands. "Personal letters of the normal kind. The one still in the bag is a bundle of letters of the more unusual kind. What I mean by that is that they appear to be replies to threatening ones from Miles McMaster. All about money owed to him, though."

"Maybe that was why he was so upset when he heard that Peter Yair had died. Money owed to him not being paid and McMaster's chances of financial survival going down the stank. Maybe he didn't know at that time he was the heir?" suggested Jacobstein.

"Did any of them specify the exact nature of what the money he was due was to cover?" asked Pollock.

"Yes, Ben, they all did. Small architectural designs, very small, but they all add up to a considerable sum of money."

"Any from Yair?"

"None," replied Tiffney shaking his head as he sugared the mug of very strong tea put in front of him by Quigley.

"Cash in hand from Cousin Miles, maybe," said Jacobstein. "Miss Colquhoun didn't strike me as being the type to contemplate subsidising mates."

"Scary, is she, Jake" suggested Tiffney.

"I thought so."

"Probably because she managed to keep one step ahead of us, boys," said Pollock smiling broadly. "I don't know about you, Jake, but I left with the distinct impression we were a couple of losers. Not a good feeling."

"She's a very assertive person, Ben," remarked Jake Jacobstein. "It's all probably second nature to her. She's nobody's fool, either. The ladies in that family probably do the contract negotiations with the circus owners, and believe me, they try to strike a very hard bargain. My cousin had to negotiate a catering contract with one of them in England and he said it would have made him pennies and the owner a rich man." Heads were shaken all round.

"But my question concerning the ex-schoolteacher is this and I would like the three of you to think about it while I make some fresh tea and Austin breaks out the pastries. Give Austin first choice as the lady meant them for him. I'll send somebody up to Enzo's to replenish your stock when this is all done and dusted. Now, the question is why does Andrea Colquhoun hate Peter Yair so deeply? Discuss that amongst yourselves." With that he began to make the tea. "I'm off to have a word with Sergeant Hanley about some cake."

All crockery was washed and replaced and Pollock hoped that the interval of deep thinking would have produced something substantial. He was afraid, from the little whispered gems he had overheard, that Celtic's forward line had now been settled to the detriment of two murder investigations. Hope really did spring eternal, though, in the inspector's heart.

"So, let's have it. Even if your main ideas sound fanciful, there might be more than a grain of truth in them. It's happened before and my fingers are crossed that it'll happen again right now."

"All three individually or a spokesman, sir?" asked Quigley.

"A spokesman to begin with, Austin, and then we'll throw the discussion open." Tiffney took the floor as the most senior man there. He had been a detective sergeant for a good few years longer than Jacobstein.

"Right then, here we go. As instructed, Ben, we just let our imaginations run wild for a bit and then reduced the outrageous suggestions to ones more feasible and practical. We've finally come up with three fair reasons and we'll be expecting you to ask for evidence to back upour theories."

"Point taken, Felix." Pollock sat with his notebook and pencil ready.

"Now, the question we were asked to supply answers to was this; Why does Andrea Colquhoun hate Peter Yair? We relied on Jake to supply the reason for asking the question as he had been with you when you were investingating most aspects of this. He was most likely to know what gave you the reason for asking. Jake has said that the idea almost certainly came from not only her tone of voice when she spoke of him but also the very derogatory language she used such as loathsome, crude, swine and scum. Frankly, I've been called worse outside The Clay Pipe on a Saturday night and thought nothing of it as I regarded it as fair comment, but I'll tell you all about that at a later date, gentlemen." Fleix cleared his throat quietly then proceeded. "She made it quite plain that she didn't like him. Now, our first idea was this. Had he tried to rope her into his prostitution ring as a madam, not actually servicing men but overseeing the business which would free him up for other equally distasteful enterprises? Your turn, Ben." Pollock had been scribbling away.

"Your evidence then, Felix, and I'll give you my thoughts on the matter once you've done that."

"Nothing in the way of factual evidence. Jake says that she was furious when you mentioned Yair's involvement in prostitution. Her reply definitely sounded as if she were more than just suspecting something amiss. She was familiar with the operation, where it took place, who the participants were. Then again, she didn't confirm that she'd ever been a party to it, in fact, she inferred the opposite. Jake says she seemed to have no empathy with the plight of the girls involved. She appeared very hard and would, possibly, have been an excellent addition to his organisation in her capacity as an organiser and persuader, shall we say."

"Well thought out and I'll be happy to work along these lines. That lady could stand a bit more investigation into her business affairs."

"The second idea that made it onto our final list was this. She was obviously fond of Miles McMaster as Jake says she spoke well of him. Was she really angry at Yair for dragging McMaster down? He'd have had to leave his own wife and lifestyle and take an office job with Jardine Matheson to keep an eye on Yair. When Yair was shipped home, did McMaster become tarred with the same brush? Two bad eggs in one family? Money being the final temptation for Yair and McMaster doing the hard work of holding the family's reputation together for no real reward for being the watch-dog? Had the pressure he was under to keep tabs on the wayward cousin contributed to the physical outburst that scuppered McMaster's career? Or was Peter Yair's death in fact the result of a woman who had had enough simply losing complete control of herself when Yair refused to let McMaster lead his own life? All just ideas, Ben. Take them or leave them. Just from the way she defended McMaster when you spoke to her, says Jake. She was, he says, very emotional for such a hard woman."

"Could definitely be that, Felix. The three of you have come up with some excellent theories there. You've given me some points to work on. Now let's have the third one, Felix."

"The last one has absolutely nothing at all to back it up. It's just something Austin here thought possible. He has a very romantic side to his nature. We know from her own admission and his that Andrea Colquhoun and Nigel Rowley were having a love affair. Whether or not it's over between them, is anybody's guess. Rowley appears to have called it off quite suddenly, but still hadn't quite made up his mind that that was what he wanted. Why the letter? Now this is Quigley and his dramatic, Celtic, romantic notions running riot. Did Yair know something about Andrea Colquhoun, something sordid perhaps, which he was threatening to tell Rowley unless Andrea came to heel and helped him in his work?"

"Now that's another runner. God, where do we start?" said Pollock, putting his pencil down carefully. "Right, we'll take the three of them, prioritise them, then split them between us for investigation."

"Hang on a second, Ben, for I'm not quite finished. The letters I brought over from McMaster's flat can be interpreted in many ways. For the moment, though, I think there's one we should all look at and I think it's here in a manila envelope. It's from Miss Colquhoun to Miles McMaster and was posted in Hong Kong." Tiffney pulled it out and carefully passed it to Pollock. "The gist of it is that Miss Colquhoun states that she could quite easily kill Yair for all the trouble he's caused." Pollock looked shocked, puzzled and then very solemnly and carefully extracted the sheet of expensive paper, light and delicate, from a well-thumbed envelope. A minute later, he replaced the letter and envelope back into the larger manila one, put it into his desk drawer and locked the desk.

"I think we might just put these three theories on the back burner for now. The first thing we have to do is to check Andrea Colquhoun's alibi for the evening of Peter Yair's death She says she spent it watching Miss Columbine doing her dog act. The problem is we don't know exactly when Yair was beaten up, only when he was picked up. But it seems certain, from the medical evidence, that Yair was killed on the previous evening although he was discovered dead the following morning. Now, Miss Colquhoun is an attractive lady with a lovely figure. She also has very strong arms and hands, very strong indeed. They have to be if she's working on the trapeze. Yair certainly looked fit, but if the first blows were very hard and destructive and he was taken by surprise, Miss Colquhoun could have finished him off without much bother. Whether or not she meant to kill him is not up to us to decide. We'll leave the finer points to the folk who earn the big money."

"How do we go about getting the proof or otherwise of her alibi, sir?" asked Quigley.

"You and Felix trot off to the Britannia, the music-hall. Go there and ask around. You know the ropes, Felix. Cecil Snowball and Miss Columbine are due here shortly so Jake and I will quiz them as to what they know about the alibi." Felix Tiffney and Austin Quigley left and Pollock hoped they were now on the way to solving at least one murder.

Pollock took the letter out of his desk and read it through once more.

"Here, Jake, leave your notes for a minute and read this. Seems to have been the only piece of correspondence between them in the flat." Jacobstein laughed.

"Probably in case Gina came cleaning and would wonder if anything was going on between them."

"Doesn't read like anything was going on. Read it." Jacobstein read it twice and passed it back.

"Just reads like a concerned letter from one friend to another. Interesting that she writes she's thinking of going back into the family business and he was right all along about her suitability as a teacher. I take it that this was written when she'd had the letter that made her turn back?" Pollock shook his head.

"I'm not taking that tale as gospel, the one about the relative. She got a letter alright but it was from Rowley telling her it was all off, the secondment and the romance. I'd bet my life on that. My money's on Rowley's story. He gave her up and she came back to plead with him for another chance. If we found Rowley dead, I'd know who was responsible. And what was Helen Rowley's relationship with Peter Yair?"

"He seems to have been the controlling figure in all of this," asnswered Jacobstein.

"By virtue of his excessive charm and expectations of money. Was he also capable of putting the thumbscrews on when he was thwarted?" Both men sighed and hoped that their next two visitors would be a bit more forthcoming and precise about Yair, McMaster and Miss Colquhoun. It seemed to Pollock that Miss Columbine had been leading him up the garden path with the last person. Or had Andrea Colquhoun simply slipped into the Britannia and out again without telling Miss Columbine she had been there?

"We've a lot riding on Mr Snowball and Miss Columbine, Ben. It seems to me that they could put us onto the right trail or stymie the whole enquiry."

"I know, Jake. It's come to a poor pass when we're relying on a third-rate riveter and a dog act." Jacobstein burst out laughing and Pollock's mood changed completely. "Still, it'll be an amusing interlude before we see the habitual liars again. If they're now here, Jake, will we tidy up this office as Miss Columbine seemed to me to be a most particular sort of person?" So saying, he swept everything off the top of his desk, after placing the letter in the long, top drawer, and into the deep drawer on the right. He then waited and hoped.

They had arrived. Pollock could hear Jacobstein chatting to Miss Columbine as they climbed the stairs. The door opened and the lady herself entered in a waft of gardenia scent and giggles. Jake must be overdoing the compliments, thought Pollock. Cecil Snowball's loud laughter followed her into the office and the inspector offered both of them tea, coffee and regretted having polished off the pastries. Two plain biscuits were all that were left and both visitors graciously accepted them. Cecil, obviously deferring to the presence of class in the form of Miss Columbine, refrained from dunking his biscuit.

"It's good of both of you to agree to helping us out today, Cecil and you, Miss Columbine."

"Our pleasure, Mr Pollock, Mr Jacobstein. The coffee is delicious and a McVitties tea biscuit never tasted better. Do you agree, Miss Columbine." Miss Columbine did. Pollock was beginning to wonder if Mr Pierot was not the jealous type or had he another Mrs Pierot tucked away somewhere and had taken his eye off the ball?

"I do, Mr Snowball, I do." Miss Columbine's nodding head scattered another miasma of gardenia and Pollock was beginning to feel slightly light-headed.

"We're really looking for some background information. Firstly, though, have you heard that Mr Yair's cousin, Mr Miles McMaster, has died?"

"We have, Inspector Pollock, a terrible piece of news. Rumour has it he committed suicide in the Necropolis." Miss Columbine exchanged sad glances with the ex-riveter. "A very likeable man in his way," she added sadly.

"And dominated by that rascal Peter Yair." Miss Columbine nodded her agreement at this state of affairs between cousins. Pollock wondered if they had ever spoken to his widow. "Mr McMaster was so considerate whenever Cecil and I, and indeed Mr Pierot too, entered that wonderful café. And to think he died so tragically and so near to the place he called home." There followed a most ladylike sniff of regret.

"More than that, I'm afraid, because it wasn't suicide."

"A dreadful accident then? Did one of those great crosses or angels topple down on him. You said they were very unsafe, didn't you Cecil, the last time we strolled through there?"

"I did and I was right, Collie. I've always said that nobody should be allowed to erect those statues. Totally unsafe. His widow should sue the authorities."

"You have always said that, Cecil," agreed his fellow-lodger.

"Have either of you ever met Mrs McMaster?" asked Jacobstein, looking from one to the other.

"I haven't, no," said Miss Columbine, "well, not as yet but we intend to call in at the café and pay our respects and condolences, don't we?" Mr Snowball nodded his agreement. "The lady must be devastated by this."

"Mr McMaster was murdered, I'm afraid," said Pollock, really in order to avoid agreeing about the devastation that Gina was definitely not feeling.

"Mudered?" Both Miss Columbine and Mr Snowball sounded and looked shocked, shocked into near silence , it seemed.

"Is that possible?" asked Mr Snowball softly as if the ghost of McMaster might hear him and object to being discussed.

"I'm afraid it is. More coffee, Miss Columbine?" asked Jacobstein quietly. But the lady merely shook her head slowly.

"I think I'll move on from Bosworth Street, Cecil." Cecil nodded having let go of his new career as a landlord.

"Me too, Collie." Pollock was only too aware that he had brought, what was for the two unusual characters before him a happy outing, to a calamitous end. He moved on, too.

"What we'd like to know from you is a little more about Mr McMaster as a person and also his relationship with Peter Yair."

"I think, Collie, you know more about him than I do as you've lived there longer than I have." The lady took up the story.

"I know they were cousins for Peter Yair told me. They were also business partners in a way. Yair was the dominant one. As he left the house, Mr McMaster would always wave to me in the sitting-room or if I were at the window. A shy man in company, I suspect, a bit awkward perhaps, but very pleasant. I think he was Peter Yair's errand boy for he would sometimes say as he left the house that his life was full of errands and that he should have taken up my offer to teach him how to ride a bicycle all those years ago. A soft sort of humour. Dreadful tragedy his death is. He seemed lately to be getting back into his architectural niche, so to speak. It's a great pity for he seemed to be so well respected."

"We'll do our best to discover who did it, I can assure you of that." Jacobstein kept his head well down over his notebook as his boss spoke. Cecil Snowball gently patted Miss Columbine's hand in a very sensitive way.

"I suppose bringing a killer to justice is some comfort not only to the victim's family but to society at large, Inspector Pollock. We'll do all we can to help." Mr Snowball nodded his agreement.

"It's also our duty, of course, to find out who Peter Yair's killer is. He seems to have led the kind of life where enemies were almost inevitable."

"You can say that again," said Mr Snowball. "I suppose some people with money, instead of being content and grateful, want more and it tends to lead them into bad company."

"Cecil, dear, I think Mr Yair would be the bad company in any group."

"I think you're right, Collie, but everybody has a right to live."

"And what was your impression of Mr Yair, Miss Columbine." That lady sighed deeply.

"He was a very unpleasant and inconsiderate man, really. Hadn't paid a bill, I'm told, since he took over the house. Always cold, it was, and the cooking just didn't have the high standards it used to. We now have to buy our own food or eat out, don't we Cecil?" Her friend nodded wisely. "Yes, he might have had plenty of money, but he kept it all to himself, so Mr McMaster told me in confidence. That was after they'd had that terrific row. You remember that, Cecil?"

"Colossal row!"

"Mr McMaster was almost in tears as he spoke to me later. He was terribly upset or he would have said nothing about his cousin at all. That was his way."

"And then Yair appeared and he was all sweetness and light, wasn't he, Collie? Blamed it all on Mr McMaster but said he couldn't help it. It had been family bad news and Mr McMaster couldn't handle the grief and shock, that's what Yair said, Inspector Pollock." The ex-riveter bristled with annoyance.

"Now I wonder if I could ask you, Miss Columbine, a few questions about Miss Andrea Colquhoun."

"Ask away, inspector, for we're here to help you." Another quick bit of nodding and gardenia filled the air again. Pollock's thoughts were swept back to India for a brief moment.

"First of all, thank you for the address you gave us. It has proved to be very helpful. We have now spoken to Miss Colquhoun and she was most anxious to help. We asked her about the two gentlemen, Yair and McMaster, as she knew both of them in Hong Kong for a short time. I must say that her assessment of their characters agrees with yours."

"Apart from when she visited and saw Mr Yair, have you seen her more recently?" The lady thought long and hard before shaking her head.

"No, I haven't. Wait, I think I did see her quite recently at the Britannia. Could be wrong, though, as it was only for a fleeting moment. Andrea and I always got on well together. I'm actually rather fond of her." Not too fond to lie for her, hoped Ben Pollock.

"Do you remember exactly when, Miss Columbine? We have to check everybody's whereabouts."

"Including mine and Cecil's? That's part of your job, inspector. Let me think. Very recently but when exactly?" She laughed suddenly. "Monday or Tuesday of this week. Can't remember exactly but it certainly wasn't Wednesday because that was my birthday and Cecil took me out to dinner. Some of my fox terriers were off-colour, shall we say, and the theatre owner didn't want to take the chance that there might be some excrement lying on stage when we were finished. We all had the night off and Mr Pierot too the little fellows back home."

Jacobstein showed Miss Columbine and Mr Snowball out and came back with a grin that said he'd won that metaphorical watch.

"So she wasn't there, Jake, she wasn't there, the little liar. But where exactly was she, Jake?"

"Would you really like to know, Ben, or do you want to wait until Felix and Austin come back with their report to confirm it?"

"So you know something I don't, Jake? But how could you? Sergeant Hanley?" Jacobstein nodded.

"The constable you were speaking to today in Alloa Street."

"Angus McCallum! That's his name!"

"Well, Angus McCallum just popped in to say that one of the Reverend Carson's church members met Miss Andrea Colquhoun running out of Lavender Street and threatened to beat her up if she ever mentioned meeting here there that night."

"Got her!"

Chapter 10

Pollock and Jacobstein waited anxiously for news from any of the dozen or so policemen and detectives scouring the East End and farther afield for any sign of Andrea Colquhoun. A quick sketch by Jacobstein supplemented by drawings of her from a circus programme were all most of them had to go on to identify her.

"They'll bring her mother in if she's the least bit unco-operative. That woman will be a hard nut to crack for any information, Jake."

"Maybe she won't be as this is so serious. She's got her entire family to think of. Besides, publicity is all that matters and she'll be anxious to avoid any more murders than can be helped, Ben."

"I wonder what this is really all about? That group in Hong Kong. What was it really doing, what were they all up to? They didn't all come rolling back home in the money, so what was it all about?"

"It beats me," said Jacobstein, shaking his head ruefully. "Do you mind if I open a window, Ben? This place still reeks of Miss Columbine."

"It doesn't reek, Jake. That's the scent of gardenia. Too exotic for you, my lad. I'll bet Gina will fall at your feet if you gave her a bottle of it."

"I'll make a note of that," said the sergeant sarcastically, but his voice was laced with just a hint of interest.

The door was suddenly opened after a very peremptory knock and Hanley entered.

"Got a gentleman downstairs who would like a word with you, Ben. Or actually, he seems to be of the opinion that you wanted a word with him. He's an army sergeant by the name of Rowley."

"Jake, would you bring him right up. Thanks, Bill. Any interesting news for us yet?" Pollock asked hopefully.

"Sorry, Ben, nothing at all." Hanley and Jacobstein left and Pollock waited with barely suppressed excitement for Rowley to appear. There were so many questions that needed to be answered and he was certain Rowley could fill in many blanks in their case. The door opened and Rowley was shown to a chair by the desk where Pollock sat.

"Good of you to come, Sergeant Rowley. We'd like you to answer a few more questions, if you don't mind, ones that are bothering us right now. They're not strictly about yourself and maybe just more opinions than actual fact. We're building character sketches and there are, at the moment, a few blanks. We're confident that you'll be able to complete the pictures for us."

"I'll certainly do my best, Inspector Pollock. I'd like to put all of this behind me and move on."

"Then let's not waste any time. Now, down to business. Can you tell me what were the circumstances that led to you meeting the others in that group in Hong Kong? With Peter Yair, Miles McMaster and Andrea Colquhoun?"

"There was no real common interest. My wife and I were out strolling, looking at some Chinese boats in the bay, went into an hotel for some tea and the others were already there. It was a bit crowded so they let us share their table. The men said they worked for Jardine Matheson and Andrea was with a circus that had just arrived a short time before. Yair and McMaster were cousins and Andrea had known them from home. The men were lovers of the theatre and circus, that sort of entertainment. Helen was fascinated by Andrea being a trapeze artist and acrobat and it all led on from there – social outings and the like."

"And you fell for Andrea?"

"More or less. She's an educated woman, a teacher as you know. Looks and brains. That appealed to me."

"And your wife, did she find the men interesting?"

"Not especially. She wasn't that type. She was married and that was that." Pollock nodded sagely.

"Now, if we could turn to Peter Yair. I know we mentioned that gentleman the last time we spoke, but we really learned nothing about him. I maybe asked the wrong questions, Sergeant Rowley. Perhaps this time, I could help you do a little more in-depth thinking about him." Rowley shrugged.

"What is there to say? He was a great man who was in love with my wife but was far too honourable to make a play for her. Instead, he became her best friend and confidant. I wasn't, and at that point, I didn't care."

"You had other interests?"

"Yes."

"This honourable character. What exactly does than mean? Did he hold the door open for the ladies?" Rowley smiled slightly.

"Of course, he did."

"Then we're all honourable men, sergeant. Even some of the most dishonourable men I've met through this job are honourable ones by your standards."

"Yair was just an exceptionally fair-minded person who was much put upon by that degenerate cousin of his."

"The cousin being Miles McMaster?"

"The very same." Jacobstein wanted to turn the clock back a few days and start all over again.

"Now that surprises me, Sergeant Rowley, for that summary of Peter Yair's character is the complete reverse of what I've been led, so far, to believe," said Pollock, slightly puzzled. Rowley shrugged yet again and leaned forward in his chair. His voice was very quiet when he spoke.

"I can't help who you've been listening to, Inspector Pollock, or what you've been hearing, but I'm right and you're wrong. That is one soldier's word to another." Pollock thought about it for a second or two.

"And I accept that, Sergeant Rowley."

"Peter Yair's life was one of total misery. He was in Hong Kong simply to put the brakes on Miles McMaster, to extricate that bit of shit from every decadent and degrading situation he revelled in."

"Like what?"

"Drugs, the black market, simple fraud and, of course, prostitution. McMaster indulged in the latter from the moment he landed in Hong Kong and eventually ran a little operation of his own. It was very little by the standards out there but big enough to force Peter to bail him out and leave the place in one helluva hurry. He had made it to Hong Kong in a bid for escapism but his aunt begged him to get a job for McMaster and the soft fool did."

"Did Yair tell you this?"

"No chance. He was like a clam. A lovely, friendly, cheery type who saw the best in everybody. It was another Jardine Matheson employee who told me when he was half-drunk and loose-tongued. Peter was well-liked and his friends resented the way his life was going down the drain. But he wouldn't listen to them when they told him to get rid of the slug. That man who told me was related distantly but he kept well away from that archetypal sponger, McMaster. Amoral is the best word to describe him."

"He's dead!" Surprise showed briefly on the soldier's face.

"No loss to the human race."

"Murdered!" Rowley grinned slightly at this information from Pollock.

"Well, Inspector Pollock, he lasted longer than he should have. There'll be nobody mourning his departing this life."

"Andrea Colquhoun, maybe?" Pollock suggested.

"Hardly," was Rowley's sarcastic response.

"I'll be quite honest with you, sir, several people have given us a completely different idea of Mr McMaster and his lifestyle and that includes his relationship with his cousin."

"Then you've been consorting with liars and, if I were you, I'd check up and see what their motives are for skewing your enquiries." Pollock and Jacobstein were beginning to wonder that, too, so convincing was the soldier.

"Miss Colquhoun's assessment of both men's characters is radically different from yours and she's backed up by other independent people we've interviewed. Now, if you're right."

"And I am," interrupted the sergeant.

"And she's wrong," continued Pollock, "how does that come about?"

"I've no idea for she was a friend of Peter Yair's. She had very little to do with Miles McMaster as far as I know."

"And what form did that friendship take, do you know?"

"Religion. Oddly enough, Andrea is genuinely interested in mission work. Not missionary work. She got herself involved in that kind of thing wherever the circus landed."

"And she did it in Hong Kong?"

"That's right. She introduced Peter to her religious friends and it took over his life. He definitely had his heart set on it until." Rowley suddenly stopped talking.

"Until what?" asked Pollock.

"Until he fell for Helen. Then it slowly changed into social projects at home. He was a very good-living man, Inspector Pollock and nothing can ever change that no matter who says otherwise."

"But Miles McMaster was his heir?" The soldier shook his head.

"Not so, inspector, for he untended leaving his entire estate to charity or so Helen told me. While we were still in Hong Kong."

"Tell me, Sergeant Rowley, why would Andrea Colquhoun hate Peter Yair so much?" The sergeant simply shook his head.

"Now to that question, Inspector Pollock, I have no answer. Andrea is a very complex character, lots of emotion, fiery, and at times, bitter if she doesn't get her own way. That is very wearing to be constantly subjected to and a man burns out very quickly close to her. It's a relief to finally move on."

"Just a last question, Sergeant Rowley. Why did you really break it off with Miss Colquhoun?" Rowley gave in.

"Peter Yair got in touch with me saying that Andrea had written letters to Helen threatening to kill her if she didn't stay away from me. It was all in her mind. Peter knew about it from Helen. Here's a letter he gave me that was written by Andrea." He passed it over to Pollock who read it and frowned.

"May I keep it, sergeant?"

"You might as well as Helen and Peter are both dead now. There's nobody to return it to now."

"By the way, Sergeant Rowley, don't suppose you gave Miss Colquhoun any little souvenirs of your relationship, by any chance, that only a soldier, shall we say, might possess? A little piece of a firearm?" Rowley frowned then laughed.

"Dumped it, did she? Her idea, inspector, not mine. A small bit of a museum piece I kept as a lucky charm. She saw it and wanted it. Think I'll settle for a good book for a while and leave the ladies alone." Something inside Pollock's head rang like the proverbial bell.

"You're a reader, are you?" Rowley nodded.

"Always have been."

"Use a bookmark, do you?" Rowley laughed.

"Can't be doing with them. A torn bit of the Daily Record is good enough for me. Oddly enough, Andrea should have been being a teacher, but wasn't. Once gave me a lovely embroidered, Chinese bookmark with a tiger on it. I passed it on to Helen. Was more her style." With that, Nigel Rowley shook hands with both Pollock and Jacobstein and left.

"He should have stuck to the Sergeants' Mess," was Pollock's only cryptic comment before sitting down again.

"My head's reeling, Jake."

"What was that last bit all about, Ben?" asked Jacobstein puzzled.

"Sergeant Rowley has just told us who trashed Peter Yair's flat. So, Jake, where are we now and don't say up a creek without a paddle? Who's telling the truth?"

"Gina Brossi!"

"Wish I'd put money on your saying that," said Pollock laughing.

"All right, Gina and the sergeant."

"So why has Andrea and the residents of Bosworth Street told us otherwise and where the hell is that woman? Also, why the long silence from the Celtic supporters? Aw, don't bother answering that last one."

"Alright, Ben, where are we? This is how it looks to me. We have a sudden death, Helen Rowley. Since we really don't now much about her, we've knocked it off as it turns out her death was due to natural causes. That leaves us with two very unnatural deaths, those of Peter Yair and his cousin, Miles McMaster."

"Suspects?" asked Pollock.

"Mainly one – Miss Andrea Colquhoun, trapeze artist, school-teacher and, quite possibly, a first-rate liar," said Jake.

"Very true. And the evidence for the need for our continuing search for this lady?" asked Pollock.

"She was seen emerging from the street where Peter Yair met his untimely death on the same evening and threatened a witness with extreme violence. She also hated Peter Yair although they were close at one time." Jacobstein looked quickly through his notebook again. "And that's about it for Peter Yair's murder. Miles McMaster's is wide open. All we know is that somebody hoisted him up after applying a specialised hold to his neck in order to render him unconscious."

"I don't see any connection with Miss Colquhoun anymore than anyone else except that she is an exceptionally strong woman and for reasons best known to herself, she tells us how wonderful McMaster was," said Pollock sceptically. "My own impression of the man would be more likely to agree with Rowley and Gina. There was definitely more to McMaster than met the eye."

"Cultivated the vacant look?" Jacobstein suggested wryly.

"Didn't do him any harm did it? Well, not in the short-term anyway. Lived off the aunt, Peter Yair and your Gina."

"Miss Gina Brossi," Jacbstein said archly. Pollock laughed.

"Somehow I don't think you'll have much chasing to do there, Jake, for if that particular lady decides you're for her, you'd better batten down the hatches or just give in right away." As always, Jacobstein decided to just grin and bear it.

"I think I hear our own Celtic brake club heading up the stairs," he said, deftly switching the subject.

"With a certain lady, I hope," Pollock added, stood up and dusted himself down.

The door opened and Miss Andrea Colquhoun was shown in by Felix Tiffney. Austin Quigley thought the office looked a bit crowded and decided to linger in the corridor and wait for further developments. Miss Colquhoun accepted the offer of a chair by Pollock but refused the offer of tea.

"Thank you for coming in, Miss Colquhoun," said Pollock smiling and sitting down at the desk.

"Didn't have much choice, did I?"

"Actually, no. But we sometimes have to use slightly more persuasive methods for not everyone is as co-operative as you, Miss Colquhoun."

"Please come to the point. I have business to attend to."

"As have we, madam, and this is it. Two murders to solve, to be precise."

"I don't see how I can possibly be of any more help to you, Inspector Pollock."

"I can assure you there is always a little something most of the people we interview have forgotten to tell us. By the way, there will be no objection from us if you would prefer to wait until a legal representative is here acting on your behalf." She waved that one away.

"No doubt most of them like a second interview here if only to enjoy the pastries while you're conducting it." Everyone's eyes followed hers down to the carpet and a small pile of pastry flakes.

"Lunch-time, I'm afraid," lied Pollock as Tiffney kicked it under the desk.

"Out of sight," Tiffney intoned, "out of mind. Man cannot live by bread alone, miss."

"He could try," said Miss Colquhoun, the schoolteacher, dryly. "I take it that Gina Brossi has been here and that was her calling card? Mine is not nearly so satisfying but more truthful, I suspect."

"That will definitely be a change," said Pollock, now siding with the doubting Jacobstein.

"And that means precisely what, Inspector Pollock?"

"Quite simply that you've off-loaded a pile of lies on us, Miss Colquhoun." Pollock threw that out and waited.

"Try and be a little more explicit, please."

"Your – what should I call it? – appraisal, yes, your appraisal of Peter Yair's character was totally incorrect and I would like to know why. Put briefly, and perhaps brutally, why did you hate him enough to kill him?"

"It's perfectly possible to hate someone without being tempted either to kill him or actually to do it. But I did not hate Peter nor did I kill him. I think I might have that tea now, Inspector Pollock, please. No sugar, just a spot of milk. No biscuits, thank you." That was a relief, thought Jacobstein, the empty biscuit barrel looming large in his mind's eye.

"Your occupation, your circus one I mean, must mean that you keep yourself very fit." Miss Colquhoun nodded in agreement.

"My life depends on being fit, I can assure you." Tiffney rose and whispered to Quigley as he entered the office silently then left again.

"So, Miss Colquhoun, the truth this time. I'm sure you'll get to the point quickly and stick to it." Silence reigned until Quigley fetched the tea.

"Do you really want to now the truth about Peter Yair and me?" Pollock nodded. Miss Colquhoun took a long drink of her tea which Quigley had brought in, placed the cup back very carefully in the saucer and looked Pollock straight in the eye. Her blue eyes were deep as lapis lazuli, dark pools of unfathomable feeling. "Why did I hate him? I didn't. I loved him like a brother. There was never anybody like Peter. He was kind, funny, affectionate and true. His loyalty was his great downfall and his inability to see bad in even the most evil of people."

"We have a witness who says you were in Lavender Street around the time Mr Yair was badly assaulted, an assault that led to his death."

"All right then, I killed him." Silence reigned as Pollock glanced swiftly over the pristine foolscap block in front of him.

"Why, Miss Colquhoun?" He felt oddly disappointed.

"Does it really matter? Peter's dead. You can say I killed him. That's it."

"Indulge me, Miss Colquhoun. You see, we're investigating the deaths of two cousins and those deaths might just be linked. Then again, it's just feasible that the timing of those deaths might just be co-incidental."

"I have no idea why Miles was killed or who killed him."

"Let's go back a little, if we may. Would you tell us exactly why you hated Peter Yair?"

"I did not hate Peter. I've already told you that."

"But you did kill him. There must have been a reason." He waited until she had finished her tea.

"I hit him several times. I was very angry with him."

"Why were you angry with him?"

"He was in love with Helen Rowley."

"And you were jealous?"

"Don't be absurd!" Pollock felt well and truly slapped down. "I loved him like a brother. I've already explained that. It'll all be in Sergeant Jacobstein's very neat notes. Could you open a window, please, for I'm feeling rather hot?" Pollock signalled to Tiffney and he fetched a pole and opened the top of the tall window.

"Probably the tea," suggested Pollock feebly.

"I was angry with him beyond all reason. I had asked him where Nigel Rowley was. I knew he would know because he was very close to Nigel's wife. They'd met in Hong Kong. He wouldn't tell me. He was more interested in protecting her than in helping me. The letter I told you I received in Hong Kong some months ago was from Nigel saying we were finished. He loved his wife, he wrote, and I suppose he still does. I had to see him again and the only way was through Helen. I knew he'd left the army so he could have been staying anywhere. She'd know where he was. But Peter refused to say when I met him by arrangement that evening. I lost my temper and hit him I don't know how many times. He fell to the ground and I left. I didn't know he was seriously hurt. There was no great strength in the blows I gave him or at least I thought not. I was out of my mind because I wanted to see Nigel so badly. That was the end of my beautiful Peter's life and mine." There was a sorrowing silence from her then and none of the men there knew how to break it. "Is there anything else, Inspector Pollock?" Pollock knew he would have to charge her with her friend's death.

"Just one or two more questions, Miss Colquhoun. First, though, you do realise we'll have to charge you with Peter Yair's death?" Miss Colquhoun bowed her head slightly. "You'll need a solicitor, now." She nodded again but said nothing. “Shall we summon him before we go any farther with our questions?” She wrote down his name and address.

“There’s no need to wait for him coming. What do you want to know?”

“The questions are mainly about Miles McMaster. It seems to me that you deliberately swapped the cousins’ characters, am I right?”

“Yes.”

“Why? We’re investigating Mr McMaster’s death so I would strongly advise you not to answer my questions if you think they might incriminate you or simply wait until your solicitor arrives and answer only if he advises you to do so.”

“Thank you but I know my own business best. Besides, the solicitor is my half-brother and he’s not very competent. Should have stuck to the trapeze. His selling point is he’s cheap and a first-rate singing clown. He probably won’t win your case but he’ll certainly keep you entertained.” Tiffney lost control of his grin and received a thundering scowl from his boss. Pollock felt like a worm, but there were answers that were essential in solving the McMaster case only Andrea Colquhoun would know.

“Why did you switch the cousins’ personalities, Miss Colquhoun?” She gave him a most seductive smile.

“I’ll deviate a little, Inspector Pollock, if I may.” Pollock nodded and waited. “Mrs McMaster, the tornado of Enzo’s café, had Miles nailed, in a manner of speaking. No doubt she had a great many colourful adjectives to describe her husband, but I’ll just use one today. Degraded. He was a very degraded human being. He was everything that I told you Peter was and vice versa. When I learned that Peter was dead, he appeared and told me he knew I was responsible. He had seen it all. He had blackmail in mind when he suggested that I run his prostitution business. There were no depths to which he wouldn’t stoop. If ever a man deserved to die, it was Miles McMaster.”

“I take it it was you who trashed Peter Yair’s room?”

"Yes, it was. Miles said that he had written the details of Peter's death in a letter which he had left in a secret place in Peter's room. I had to get that letter. Actually, Miles was only doing what Miles always did best, manipulating people, controlling them. I don't think he had seen anything. I'd told him I was meeting Peter and he just guessed the rest. I don't think there ever was a letter." Pollock let it go at that. He would settle for charging her with Peter Yair's murder and deal with McMaster's later. Somehow he felt emotionally drained. Jacobstein and Tiffney did not look any too great either. Austin Quigley put his head round the door, signalled to him and Pollock slipped silently out. Seconds later, he returned and spoke to Tiffney.
"Miss Colquhoun, DS Tiffney and DC Quigley will now take you downstairs. Once your solicitor has arrived, DS Tiffney will charge you with the murder of Peter Yair." Andrea Colquhoun nodded to each of the detectives there in turn and walked out with Felix Tiffney.

Pollock and Jacobstein entered the busy café and watched and waited while Gina served plates of creamy pasta to a table of office workers. It was a beautiful café, fine scenes of Italy vying for space on the walls with beautiful, mosaic-framed, sparkling mirrors. Pollock wondered yet again why they had had to take a cab to get there after the urgent call from Gina.
"It's my mother." Gina was not given to making long speeches. Pollock hoped Carla had not been found dead – at least not in suspicious circumstances.
"She's dead?" asked Jacobstein, his voice full of solace, at least he hoped it sounded like that.
"Do you ever have anything else on your mind?" Jacobstein blushed and Pollock grinned. Gina gave both of them a very crushing look of contempt.
"What about Mrs Brossi?" Pollock asked. Truth to tell, he had just collared one killer and the next murder had taken over. Somehow Enzo's didn't seem like a murder victim's

place of work. But he was glad to be away from the cramped Camlachie office for a while breathing fresh air and smelling Enzo's delicious coffee.

"No, not my mother. She's gone after Miss Columbine and Mr Snowball. She thinks they've gone slightly mad. Forgot to pay for their ice-cream and that's definitely not like them. What kept you so long?" Pollock took a deep breath before answering the woman who might just marry his sergeant and he himself might just be the groom's best man.

"We were in the middle of a very important interview and then had to have a word with my superintendent. About a murder. Not as important as customers legging it not paying their ice-cream bill, but that's life in the CID. Took a while but we're here now."

"Did she really do it? Andrea Colquhoun? Kill Peter Yair? I don't believe it for she was very fond of him." It seemed to Pollock that the entire world's business passed through that café. He ignored the questions.

"Alright, where did they go?"

"Miss Columbine hopped on a tram. She could be half-way to anywhere by now, though."

"Mrs McMaster," said Pollock sternly, "this is a matter for the uniformed branch not the CID. We only came because we know how upset you and your family must be at the death, very recent death, of your husband." Another crushing look. "So where are Carla and Mr Snowball?"

"They're in the Necropolis. She's just sent a boy back with a message telling me that." Something jolted in Pollock's brain and he saw that Jacobstein had had the same thought for he was already running out the door and on through the heavy traffic flowing relentlessly along the High Street. He now had Pollock on his heels, dodging the traffic as it careered relentlessly down towards The Trongate.

Cecil Snowball was balanced deftly on top of the Celtic cross that had seen Miles McMaster's body swaying lifeless from it some hours before.

"I've been waiting for you, Inspector Pollock. Got a few things to tell you. The first you can probably guess."

"Come on, Cecil, come on down and we can talk. Sit on this table gravestone for I'm getting dizzy looking up at you."

"Won't take a minute, son, and I'm not likely to fall. The riveting job, you know. Never was afraid of heights, not that you could call this high. You see, inspector, Miss Columbine and I are old friends. Both from circus families only I decided to seek my fortune in the big, wide world and finished up a riveter. Smart choice, eh? But this is really my place, up in the air, free as a bird. It was the tightrope we specialised in, my family business, so to speak. The Mondanti Brothers. All gone now. Right name was Snowball. I knew that Carla here would chase me and then send for you. I've got one or two more things to tell you."

"Come down and do it, Cecil, please."

"Sorry, Mr Pollock, I'm more at home up here balancing. Should never have left it. But there you are. Now Inspector Pollock and you, Mr Jacobstein. By the way, I love the fish and chips, bread and butter and tea in your lovely restaurant, Mr Jacobstein. Beats yours into a cocked hat, Carla." Carla fumed silently and weighed the chances of her managing to drag Mr Snowball down and giving him a good few, well-aimed slaps. "Anyway, just a few snippets of information, gentlemen, for your records. I got involved in all of this."

"Involved in what, Cecil?" interrupted Pollock.

"In the murders."

"Carla, do you want to leave?" asked Pollock quietly.

"No!" came the loud reply.

"First things first, though. Helen Rowley was my daughter by my first marriage. There was a divorce. She was only four so she stayed with her mother in Liverpool and took her mother's name. I thought when I saw her with Peter Yair that he was the one involved in prostitution. Andrea told us different last night, Miss Columbine and me. They were trying to help these unfortunate girls. I killed Peter Yair because I thought he'd corrupted my little girl, my Helen. I saw Andrea hit him and he fell. I just finished the job when she'd run off. I saw it all from the top of a tram. Fate, it was, that I was on that tram and passing by that side-street just then. It was over in a moment. I jumped off, ran back and killed the poor man. Unforgivable. Seems he was a great protector of Helen's. Kill's your soul, that does, Inspector Pollock." Cecil Snowball's face was now ashen but Pollock saw no way to get him down safely. "Heard all about the great architect and got him along here with the promise of investing in one of his pie-in-the-sky schemes. A mausoleum. Miss Columbine's hat somehow managed to get itself caught by the wind and landed here." Cecil Snowball winked and laughed. "Mr McMaster, who saw a considerable amount of money available, was the soul of gallantry. Got up on that plinth behind me here, reached out and I just tickled a little vein in his neck and he was out like a light. Miss Columbine's strong arms held him up, I swung the noose Collie had brought in her bag over his head and tied it round the transept and Collie let him go. When you think of it, though, I suppose it was really gravity that killed him, but Collie and I would prefer to take the blame." Cecil gently dropped some coins in Carla's direction. "Here's the money for the ice-cream, Carla. It was great." Those were Mr Snowball's last words. He launched himself off the cross and directed his flight face-first into the flat, table-top tombstone opposite. Carla threw up, Jake slumped onto the path and Pollock simply closed his eyes as Cecil's head was smashed to a bloody mass of brain, bone and gore.

Epilogue

The office felt empty although there were four detectives present. All their effects had been stowed away for the next case in the East End; replenished biscuit tin, sugar, mugs, two cups and saucers, three teaspoons, a kettle and sweeties. It was two days later and they were about to depart. The last mug of tea had been drunk, egg rolls had been eaten and pastry crumbs retrieved from under the desk.

"I really took to Miss Columbine," said Quigley sadly.

"Lovely lady, was she?" asked Tiffney, his head still reeling from the previous night's celebrations. 2-0 for Celtic. Tiffney gave Quigley a knowing look which told the detective constable that he had better return that policeman's hat or Tiffney would make sure he paid for it. High jinks, high spirits and their team had a treble trophy collection to be proud of.

"She was the best. What made her do it, sir?"

"She went out just like her lifelong friend, Cecil Snowball. Cecil went out doing his tightrope balancing act minus the tightrope and Miss Columbine being where she shouldn't have been but nothing and nobody could stop her."

"That was some height she fell." Jacobstein shivered as he spoke.

"A trapeze is always up a great height. Part of the appeal and a big part of the danger. Maybe Mrs Colquhoun could have tried to stop her, but she says she didn't know she was in the arena." Pollock's face told the truth of that one.

"What'll happen to her wee dogs, Ben?" Jacobstein was a renowned animal-lover.

"The show must go on, Jake. The dogs have left the music-hall business and re-entered the circus where the odd bit of doggy mess will be treated as an everyday occurrence. Miss Columbine left all her worldly possessions, including her fox terriers to Mr Pierot, her husband."

"We never did interview the janny, Ben," said Jacobstein leafing through his notes.

"Nor Jamie Dalbrenko neither, Jake. No worries, though, for the janny gave the Camlachie Burn Inn a miss that particular day and instead hopped it with one of the cleaners, and Dalbrenko has taken a vow of silence much to the delight of hundreds of backcourt occupants. Another one who's got religion. Andrea's charge will be a lesser one so that about wraps it up." Jake Jacobstein liked to have everything tied up as neatly as possible and asked Pollock,

"Just one remaining thing puzzles me about all this. Why was Peter Yair so cheery when the love of his life had just died?"

"Nobody will ever know but I think he'd had enough time to reflect by the time we got there and that was when his idealistic fervour kicked in. Helen was gone but her legacy to the needy would live on in him. Now, enough of all this for we have a visitor approaching. Come in, Dr Jeffrey!" called Pollock. "It's JAE's renowned restaurant for all of us and we'll let our esteemed pathologist try and find gold in his fish tea there. No staff discount required, Jake. The meal's on me."

Pollock looked round the little room with affection as they left, caught Jacobstein's eye and both wondered when they would once more need the biscuit tin.

If you have enjoyed reading *Came a Stranger* please leave a review on Amazon. Marie Rowan, welcomes any constructive feedback.

Camlachie Nights Trilogy

Death Watch (Book 1)

Vengeance is Mine (Book 2)

Other series by Marie Rowan published by Moira Brown:

Mitchell Memoranda Series

The Ranks of Death (Book 1)

The Realms of Death (Book 2)

The Rites of Death (Book 3)

Gorbals Chronicles Series

Once Upon a Murder (Book1)

Death is Murder (Book 2)

Pure Dead Murder (Book 3)

Dom Broadley Series (Young Adult)

Don't Go There! (Book 1)

Tell me the Secret (Book 2)

Printed in Great Britain
by Amazon

62317244R00098